Louise Rennison

the Taming of the TIGHTS

Tallulah Casey is set
for wild times…

First published in Great Britain in hardback
by HarperCollins Children's Books in 2013
HarperCollins Children's Books is a division of HarperCollinsPublishers Ltd,
77-85 Fulham Palace Road, Hammersmith, London, W6 8JB
This edition published in 2014
The HarperCollins website address is: www.harpercollins.co.uk

1

Copyright © Louise Rennison 2013
ISBN 978-0-00-732393-7

MIX
Paper from
responsible sources
FSC www.fsc.org   **FSC™ C007454**

FSC™ is a non-profit international organisation established to promote the
responsible management of the world's forests. Products carrying the FSC
label are independently certified to assure consumers that they come from
forests that are managed to meet the social, economic and ecological needs
of present and future generations, and other controlled sources.

Find out more about HarperCollins and the environment at
www.harpercollins.co.uk/green

CONTENTS

Dear Eagle-eyed mates,
Some of you may remember that in 'A Midsummer Tights Dream'
I hilariously (in my opinion) mentioned that my mum and sister
would not let me have the dead rabbit in Cain's hand wave its
paw bye-bye to Tallulah.
I said at the time (and I'm not wrong) that it is a tip-top comedy idea.
But oh no – my so-called family said it would make me seem 'childish' –
which clearly I am not. Anyway, I hid this book from them so
the crying rabbit is in, see page 7.
So ha ha ha ha for calling me childish.
Peace.

To my Family Tree and my Tree Sisters and Tree Brothers and
to the various saps – I mean – saplings. Also to the naughty
Skipton Flossies (Katie and Eve).
And of course to the Tree Doctors with their Tree pruning,
Tree mulching and their Tree hugging: Gillie, Lizzie, Tara,
Elorine, Clare, Cassie (actually officially a sap) and Gillon xxxx

CHAPTER 1
Filling my tights again

‒‒‒‒‒‒‒‒‒‒‒‒‒

Woo-hoo! And chug-a-lug-a-ding-dong. I'm on the train, chugging back to Dother Hall, the Theatre of Dreams.

Once more getting ready to fill my performance tights! Chasing the golden slippers of success! Preparing to let my feet bleed if necessary. That's what Sidone Beaver, our headmistress, says we must do if we want to be stars in the *thea-tah, dahlings*!!! And this term I'm going to fill my tights as much as is humanly possible!!!!

Who would have thought that I, me, Tallulah Casey, a gangly Irish person, would be back here for the autumn term at a Performing Arts College in the heart of the famous Dales of Yorkshire? Ooh, I think we're stopping at Skipley station. I'll get my case down and hop off.

Uuuumph. Jumping Jehosophat and his dad, it's bouncing down. Skipley is famous for its otters. I'm not surprised. If this rain keeps up, I'll be part otter by Wednesday.

Skipley is so proud of its otters that the station sign reads **Skipley Home of the West Riding Otter.**

But last time I was here some Yorkshire hooligan altered the sign so it read **Skipley Home of the West Riding Botty.**

Honestly...

I am squelching across towards it. That's where Cain was standing when I left at the end of last term. Cain Hinchcliff. Local bad boy made... er, bad.

I remember him winking at me as the train pulled out. With his dark hair whipping around his face and his dark eyes looking and looking at me. Licking his lips. Holding a dead rabbit in his hand. Making the dead rabbit he had in his hand wave its paw at me. And rub its eye with its paw as if it was crying.

He thinks that kind of thing is funny.

I dragged my case along the platform towards the sign. I hope it's been cleaned up because it doesn't give a very good impression of the... Hang on a minute, the hooligan has been at it again! Now the sign reads **Skipley Home of the Brest Riding Otter**.

That is just wrong.

That shouldn't be allowed.

What if American people were on the train? They have a seizure if you say prat.

I left the station and trundled across the bridge to catch the bus to Heckmondwhite. Brrr, I am absolutely soaking now. The rain has got in through the front of my anorak and jumper and into my new bra. Or new 'corker holder' as me and my friends say. I hope my corkers don't shrink.

Hahahaha. What larks! I'm going to put 'corker shrinking' in my Performance Art Diary, or as I call it, my 'Darkly Demanding Damson Diary'. Under 'Ideas for Modern Dance'.

A bus flew round the bend and screeched to a halt. The warm, welcoming bus opening its welcoming doors to welcome me back to my...

A cloud of smoke billowed out. The driver was smoking a pipe. Uh-oh, I recognised that balaclava. It belonged to Mrs Bottomley. She did part-time bus driving as well as cage fighting in Leeds. I said, "Single to Heckmondwhite, please."

Mrs Bottomley repeated 'single to Heckmondwhite, please' in a horrible posh simpering way as she slammed the ticket down. Then she said, looking down at my legs, "Keep those bloody legs off my seats AND mind how you go!"

She accelerated violently before I had time to sit down and I fell onto the lap of a bloke with a guide dog.

I said, "I'm really sorry but the bus…"

He said, "Is it full then, the bus? Is there nowhere else to sit? You're a bloody big lad. My legs'll be numb by the time we get to Heckmondwhite."

At a red traffic light I staggered to a spare seat.

Everyone on the bus was looking at me and grumbling. "From that bloody Dither Hall", "simpleton, I think", "they're allus messing about in beards and tights. Sitting on blind people's knees… bloody daft."

It was raining so hard you couldn't see the road ahead. It didn't make Mrs Bottomley slow down though. There was a bump and I thought I saw a sheep fly past the window, but I can't be sure. Then as we passed Grimbottom Peak it stopped raining and a watery sun came out and a little rainbow appeared.

Oooooooh, maybe the rainbow was a sign.

A sign that everything was going to be all right. All of my hopes and dreams would come true. I'd become a star but, more importantly, get a proper boyfriend. Oh, and also I'd have a corker growth spurt. Not just one corker. Both, I mean.

When we stopped at my bus stop, Mrs Bottomley was cleaning her nails with a penknife. She didn't look up as I got off but she said, "Our Beverley dun't like thee, so that meks me not like thee. Watch your sen, lady. Walls have ears and radishes repeat."

I got my case down from the bus and there before me was Heckmondwhite in all its glory! The autumnal light shining on the bus stop! The village green! The shop! The church! And the pub – The Blind Pig.

My substitute parents the Dobbins, who I lodge with in term time, are away on a Young Christians' Foraging weekend in Blubberhouses.

Harold and Dibdobs and the lunatic twins are nice but possibly the maddest people I have ever met. They're away till tomorrow so I'm staying the night with my little mate Ruby at The Blind

Pig. I'm really looking forward to seeing my fun-sized pal and her bulldog Matilda. Ruby told me that out of eighty breeds given an intelligence test, bulldogs come seventy-eighth. But that's the intelligence-o-meter test not the love-o-meter test which Matilda would definitely win paws down.

What I am not looking forward to is seeing Mr Barraclough, Ruby's dad. He's the landlord of the pub but mostly chief tormentor of me and my legs – which I must admit sometimes have a life of their own. When I am nervous or excited they, my legs, well, they initiate Irish dancing. All by themselves. My brain has nothing to do with it. Also, because of my skinniness, Mr Barraclough keeps pretending I am a long lanky lad. In a dress.

In a nutshell, Mr Barraclough and most of the village people think that Dother Hall is for fools. That's why they call it Dither Hall.

I went quietly in through the front door of the pub. There's a real racket coming from the bar so I'll just creepy creep up the stairs to Ruby's room.

"Well, well, well, thank the Lord the thespians

are back!!! I haven't known WHAT to do with myself since tha left. By 'eck, is there a giant gene in your family, young man? You've sprung up again, haven't you, lad! What are you practising being today? Dun't tell me! Let me guess." Oh dear. There he was. Ruby's dad. In his leather trousers and Viking helmet.

He was looking at me, stroking his chin.

"Hmmm. Green trousers, rain hat, anorak. Big boots. Are you a Hobbit, is that it?"

I said, "Hello, Mr Barraclough."

He put his hand to his ear. "Is that elfin you're speaking?"

Just then Bob, the technician from Dother Hall, emerged from the 'Stags' door. He was also wearing a Viking helmet. Over his ponytail. He saw me and said, "Nice one, Tallulah. Great to see you back. Monday I'll be there at Dother Hall, the dude with the know-how, the equipment king, the 'facilitator'... but tonight I'm the real me. The muso. The rhythm master. Be prepared for total madness. The vibe is going to be like awesome."

Like awesome?

He went off into the front bar.

I said, "Why is Bob here?"

Mr Barraclough chucked me under the chin.

"Why is Bob here? Why is Bob here? I'll tell you why he's here, young man. He's our new drummer for The Iron Pies. We are going to be a sound sensation. Good to see you back, young Bilbo."

He went off into the bar shouting, "Hit it, lads!"

And an awful din of drums and guitars started up. It really did sound like Bob was just hitting things.

Ruby and Matilda came tumbling down from upstairs. Matilda was leaping up at my legs and Ruby was dancing around me, yelling, "It's Tallulah-lebulla, Matilda, let's mek her dance, do the dance, Tallulah-lebulla, do the dance!!!"

I said with dignity, "I don't want to, you know I've sort of grown out of the Irish dancing thing."

The Iron Pies crashed into their version of a James Bond theme. Mr Barraclough started singing, *"From Russia with PIES I came to yooooooo."*

And Ruby had to yell over the top of it. "Oh, come on, just a little bit. For me! I'll sing the Irish song. Hiddly diddly diddly diddle."

So I let myself go. I did my Irish dancing. Ruby joined in and we were leaping and hopping around in the hallway. It was fun actually. There was no one to see me and I needed to relax so I let my knees go wherever they pleased.

When I was mid-hiddly, I noticed Matilda had got caught in the umbrella stand. Umbrellas were crashing around her. She looked up blinking at us. Ruby said, "What? What? Why are you blinking at me?'"

Then Matilda looked at the door and back at Ruby.

Ruby said, "No, I'm not taking you out now, it's quiet time."

Matilda started making a snuffling noise which sounded a bit like crying. Ruby gave in and picked her up.

"Oh, bloody hell, all right, Matilda, you daft ninny. Come on, I'll tek you out, even though it's going to be a tornado out there. C'mon, Lullah."

She rammed a hat and coat on and dragged me outside with her. For an eleven year-old she's quite strong.

Big black clouds were tumbling in again from Grimbottom and in the distance we could see lightning crackling. There was a rumble as we set off up the back path.

We reached the old tree with its branch that we sit on. Ruby pulled her coat round her and shouted above the gathering wind. "It'll start pouring down in abaht five minutes so 'go fetch!' Matilda." And Ruby flung a stick for Matilda to chase.

Matilda lay down like a splayed chicken.

Ruby said, "Oh, you!!! That's not 'go fetch', is it? That's lying down and dying for England!!!"

Ruby went running off into the bracken to get the stick, shouting, "And then you can start telling me abaht snogging and stuff, Lullah!"

Matilda's not interested in stick fetching. She knows a stick is not a biscuit so why would she want to fetch it?

Gosh, it was wild up there with the lowering sky and the trees bending in the wind and the moors stretching off.

I sat down on the branch and snuggled into my anorak and put my hood up. I was sitting on the branch that HE had sat on.

I could feel his warm presence even through my anorak.

Alex the Good.

I was sitting where Alex the Good sat.

In a way, I was sitting on his knee.

Alex, Alex the Good. Ruby's gorgey older brother.

I've got a bit of a crush on him. Even though he thinks I'm just a schoolgirl, he's always nice to me. Really specially nice to me.

He's not like the Hinchcliff brothers, Seth, Ruben and the other brother. Whose name I will never mention again. But the one who waved a dead rabbit's paw. That one.

Yes, Alex is always nice to me, encouraging me

to fill my tights. Not like Dr Lightowler the drama tutor who says, "Seeing you onstage makes me feel physically sick."

Mmmmmm, Alex.

It was sunny when I last saw him, he was up here looking out to the moors. Like Mr Darcy. Only not in pantaloons and a ruffled shirt. He saw me and said, "Hey, Lullah!" and hugged me.

In a proper huggy way. I felt myself melt. I don't mean I actually melted, I just mean... anyway, it doesn't matter whether I melted or not. It was just me and him in Brontë country. Where Em Brontë wrote *Withering Tights*. It was a perfect opportunity for him to kiss me.

But then 'she' came wafting out of a field like a, like a twit. A twit in a floaty dress. He introduced us: "Meet Candice, she's at college with me." Then he kissed her on the lips.

Do boys like twits in floaty dresses? I haven't asked Cousin Georgia that. She's told me some number one rules that they do like. Boys, I mean.

Like when you want them to like you, you have to have 'sticky eyes'. Not eyes with glue on, just eyes that do 'looking up, looking down and then just looking, full-on looking at them'.

Georgia said you mustn't accidentally do sticky eyes when a boy says something so stupid you are staring at him in disbelief. Because they will get the wrong impression and think that you actually like them. In an 'I fancy you' way.

Another top tip Georgia says is that boys like you to say nice things to them and praise them for stuff. Even if they unexpectedly do a back flip or something.

You have to say, "Golly, that's the best back flip I've ever seen."

I said to Georgia, "No fool would believe that you really liked people doing back flips."

Georgia said, "Boys will. If you say something nice to them and give them praise, they are like jelly boys and you can do anything with them."

My brother Connor thinks he is the world's top farter. Which he probably is, but I'm not going to give him praise for that. Otherwise he'd do it all day.

He does do it all day.

I've got a photo from Georgia to remind me of her. I've stuck it in my Darkly Demanding Damson Diary. It's of her and her Ace Gang sitting in one of those big teacups that go round and round at fairgrounds. They're supposed to be for tiny toddlers. In fact, there were some little children in the background crying.

On the back of the photo it says, *Send us the latest on the D. B. C. of H. Yours sincerely, A Friend. And some other friends. In our cups.*

Georgia wants the latest on the D. B. C. of H who is Cain. He's so awful I call him the Dark Black Crow of Heckmondwhite. But there won't be anything to tell Georgia because I won't be having anything to do with him.

EVER again.

Whoever *he* is.

And if I do see him, I'm going to make it clear that what happened, you know, the accidental snogging incident on the moorland path, was...

You know.

Erm, an act of madness brought on by low blood sugar.

Ruby and Matilda came bounding back. Suddenly there was a loud growling in the gorse. Ruby said hoarsely, "Maybe it's a wild otter from Skipton? Gone mad. Say something to it. Calm it down."

What do you say to otters?

Do otters go mad?

I said, "Ruby, how can it be a wild otter gone mad? You've just made that up."

Ruby said, "It's still rustling about, going to rip our throats out though, isn't it? Make friends with it."

Make friends with an otter? I called out shakily, "We come in peace, we mean you no harm."

Cain's big black dog bounded out with its tongue lolling. Cain calls his big black dog 'Dog'.

Matilda shuffled behind Ruby and me. Dog thought she was playing a hiding game. His favourite. He barked and then rushed to one side of us. Matilda quickly toddled round the other side. But then Dog unexpectedly changed direction and he came up behind and started sniffing her bottom.

Ruby shouted into the dark moors, "Cain! I know you're out there, stop messing abaht and come and get yer bloody dog. It's got its nose up Matilda's bum!"

Oh Dear Mother of Baby Jesus.

The Dark Black Crow of Heckmondwhite.

He was here.

What should I do?

I must be very cool with him.

Which is not going to be easy with my anorak hood up.

But nothing happened. There was no noise except the wind whistling and Dog sniffing.

Ruby shouted again, "Come on Cain, stop messing about."

But the moors were silent.

Then Dog cocked his ear as if he could hear something we couldn't and bounded off.

It started to pelt down, and we ran and stumbled down the hill, almost blinded by the rain.

By the time we got back to The Blind Pig, the rain was thunderous, pounding on the roof like it would break through. We got dried and had our supper in the back room. The Iron Pies were still 'rehearsing'. Well, shouting and banging.

We went up the two flights of stairs and snuggled into bed in Ruby's room high up in the attic. Matilda was tucked up at the bottom of the bed and Ruby put a little nightcap on her head. She almost immediately nodded off. Oooooh, she is sweet.

She reminds me of the owlets. Not her big puggy face and snoring, just the general feeling of lovey-doveyness.

I said to Ruby, "Hey, I'm dying to see the owlets. Shall we pop down to the barn tomorrow? Cor, I bet little Rubes and little Lullah will be pleased as anything to see us."

Ruby started plaiting her hair.

"They're not there. Connie has chucked them out. They've flown the nest."

I looked at her.

"Our little owlets have flown the nest? But…"

Ruby said, "Well, when I say 'flown' the nest, what I mean is they're crashing abaht in the woods somewhere. Tha's nivver seen such rubbish flying in your life. Little Rubes knocked herself out on the barn door the first time she tried to get out."

Our little owlets. Gone?

But they hadn't even said goodbye.

Not even, "Woo-hoo, see you later."

Ruby said, "And guess what, Beverley Bottomley has gone on hunger strike, and she says she won't stop until her mum stops stalking Cain with her shotgun."

I said, "Isn't Beverley glad about the stalking thing? She must hate Cain after what he's done to her. He's awful. He dumped her twice. And he made that song up about her called *Put your coat on, girl, you're leaving*. And the second line was '*You* were all right in the dark but then I put the light on'. At The Jones gig. He sang it straight at her. Everyone could see."

Ruby said, "I know. But she LUUUUUVES him. She thinks he's a dog wi' a bad name."

"He IS a dog with a bad name – that's because he's a bad dog."

Ruby said, "I know. But *you* let Cain the bad dog lick your nose."

Oh no, the nose-licking incident rears its head again! What would Ruby say if she knew about the accidental snogging on the moors incident?

As we lay in the dark with the wind howling and the rain sluicing down, I quickly said, "I wouldn't like to be out in this. I hope the owlets have got little owl umbrellas."

Ruby went on snuggling down. I couldn't settle though, I kept thinking about Cain.

"Do you think he saw us – Cain? Do you think he was out there with his dog, watching us?"

I shivered.

Ruby said, "Mebbe. You know those Hinchcliffs.

They can be anywhere at any time. Like a reight bad smell."

As she said that, I nearly fell out of bed because there was a massive farty noise from Matilda. It was so loud it even woke Matilda up. Ruby went mad.

"Get down, Matilda!! Bad girl, you've let yourself down AND you've let the bulldog breed down."

Matilda looked all shamefaced and tottered about on the side of the bed. She got tangled up in her nightcap and then one leg got stuck. It took so long that in the end Ruby unfastened the stuck leg and said, "Oh for goodness' sake, get in bed again. And no more trumping."

Matilda blinked sorrowfully at Ruby, who was still harrumphing about. "She hates it when I'm cross with her. Serves her right for trumping, she'll worry all night and not get any slee—"

She was interrupted by little snuffling snoring noises from Matilda.

We settled down again.

I said casually in the dark, "Have you... er,

heard how Alex, you know your brother... erm, is getting on?"

Ruby said sleepily, "Dun't start that again. Anyway, I thought you liked that Charlie?"

Ah yes, Charlie. I do like that Charlie.

The boy from Woolfe Academy for naughty boys.

But he was gorgeous. Not naughty.

Well, not very naughty.

Where's the harm in wiring up your headmaster's door handle to a minor electrical circuit? As Charlie said, "It was just high spirits, an innocent schoolboy prank."

Charlie was lovely in every way and had given me my very first proper kiss. It was dreamy but the only thing is he has a girlfriend already.

As I drifted off to sleep next to Ruby, lulled by the rain pattering on the roof, I dreamed of Charlie... Zzz

z

z

z

z

...I was up on the moorland path behind The Blind Pig. Looking through my Darkly Demanding Damson Diary. I was dressed in a black mini skirt and green tights. Thinking of doing a performance about being a person with corkers, not a silly schoolgirl any more.

Hmmmm, perhaps through the medium of dance I could show the things I'd learned from my wise Cousin Georgia.

How to do sticky eyes and 'look interested' when boys do things.

I started wafting my arms from side to side (in my dream, otherwise Ruby would have kicked me out of bed) and sweet music began floating across the moors. So lovely and magical and otherworldly, but somehow familiar.

I looked up into the tree where the music was coming from and...

...there they were, the owlets with tiny electric guitars. Hurrah!

Little Lullah was on rhythm guitar and little Rubes on bass. They were playing *Dancing Queen* by Abba!

I began to dance more wildly. Drawn by the inescapable rhythms of Sweden, lost in a world of my own.

The owlets turned up their amplifiers. (Not easy when you haven't got any hands.)

I sang my version of *Dancing Queen.*

"Friday night and it's got late
I'm out here without a mate
Got my new green tights on
You can see them from Skipton
They're in the mood for a dance
And when I get the chaaaance...
I am the dancing queen
My Irish legs have a lovely sheeeen!!!!
Oh yeah, you can dance, you can..."

And I began to spin and kick wildly, I was doing my Irish dancing on a hillock to the cool sounds of The Owlets when... Charlie! There was Charlie!

He smiled his special smile and gave a thumbs-up to the owlets. Then he danced towards me. (In time to the music, but carefully as his lurex flares were quite snug.)

Charlie looked into my eyes and then lowered his lips towards mine. Just as he'd touched my lips with his, he drew back and said (in that weird slow voice like in dreams), "No... I caaan't... I haaaaave a girlfrieeeeeend."

And he got a tiny girl out of his pocket. She waved at me.

He left with the tiny girl in his hand and sadness filled my tights. The owlets played a slow version of *Dancing Queen* on pan-pipes.

But the show must always go on. That's what Sidone tells us.

I began singing again, even though my heart was breaking.

"I am the dancing queen
My Irish legs have a lovely shhheeeeeen!!"

And someone started whistling along.

Who could this be?

Alex came up the path. In a flouncy shirt!

He danced towards me in time to the music and put his hand to my face. The frills on his sleeve temporarily blinded me. He said in a deep voice, "Hello, Tallulah, you've grown up. You are the dancing queen. Your Irish legs have a lovely sheen."

Then there was a loud growling and Cain's big black dog bounded out – ridden by Cain.

CHAPTER 2
Lullah's Lulu-luuuve List

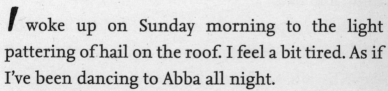

I woke up on Sunday morning to the light pattering of hail on the roof. I feel a bit tired. As if I've been dancing to Abba all night.

Rubes and Matilda were snoozing nose to nose at the bottom of the bed. So I quietly crept downstairs and unbolted the door without anyone hearing me. The church bells rang for early morning service as I crossed the village green to the Dobbins' house.

Dandelion Cottage looked sweet in the early morning hail. The trees in the garden were losing their leaves and a wisp of smoke came from the chimney. There's some ducks in the garden, but no sign of little Lullah and Ruby. I hope they're all right.

Would they even know how to build a nest? Could they catch stuff to eat?

I don't think their mum Connie has really shown them domestic skills. I've seen her eat a mouse head first, but I haven't seen her teach them grooming or home-making. Bit like my mum and dad.

When I opened the unlatched door into the kitchen, Mrs Dobbins looked up from the stove. Wearing a hat covered in dead leaves and brown stuff. She was so pleased to see me she started jumping up and down. And the hugging began immediately. She is very huggy.

"Oh, Tallulah, I have SO missed you!! You darling girl!! You've grown AGAIN!! Look at you! You are GORGEOUS. What a shame you've just missed the twins and Harold – they've gone to church. They've got Micky and Dicky with them because it's Tortoise Sunday. Ooh, we've had foraging fun, we found a badger's set. Thrilling!!! Harold followed the droppings... actually, he brought some home, I'm drying them in the airing cupboard so be careful with your undies. We're going to make sculptures with them."

I said, from underneath her arms, "That sounds, er, spiffing."

Dibdobs kissed me on the hair.

"Oooooh, you smell soooo Tallulah-ish. The twins will be so pleased to see you. Are you coming to church?"

I said, "Er, well, I'd love to but, er, I haven't got a tortoise."

Dibdobs said, "The boys would let you hold Micky and Dicky, I'm sure! Or you could take a duck."

I said quickly, "Ooooh, that would be nice, but I have to, erm, prepare myself for Dother Hall tomorrow. Check my tights and so on."

"Yes, yes, of course. I understand. Do you like my hat? It's got dried mushrooms in it."

I said, "Gosh, yes, it's spiffing. I'm just going to unpack. Toodle-pips for nowsies."

Toodle-pips?

I'd turned into Mary Poppins. I don't know why the Dobbins have that effect on me, but they do.

They are nice though, even if they're mad. It's nice to have someone so glad to see you. When I phoned Mum to tell her I'd got here last night, she didn't even know I'd gone back to college. I said, "But didn't you think it was odd that I didn't say anything? Or eat anything?"

She said, "'Oh no, I just thought you were in one of your quiet moods."

The Dobbins are not going to be back until teatime because they're going to play table tennis in Pocklington after church.

I unpacked in my old familiar squirrel room, with its window looking out over the back woods. So many memories there. The last one of Cain leaving me a poem with a knife pinning it to the old oak tree.

Huh.

He needn't think that writing a bit of a poem makes up for all those other things that I will never, ever be thinking about.

The nose-licking incident for instance or the corker-rubbing thing and the other terrible, terrible thing. That I will never, ever mention, even to myself.

I've put my private Darkly Demanding Damson Diary behind a secret panel next to my squirrel bed.

Then I had a hot chocolate and a mooch around downstairs. It looks like the lunatic twins have made a tortoise home for Micky and Dicky behind the sofa.

It can't be made out of a cabbage, can it?

Yes, it is.

By eleven, the hail had eased off so I got togged up again to look around and see if I could find the owlets. Ruby's curtains in the attic are still closed so she must be having a little lie-in.

I walked down the back path to the barn. There were no signs of life in there, just the old nest where the owlets had hatched. How sad. I shut the door and walked on past the back field.

The sheep started trying to get into the hedge when they saw me. If I didn't know for a fact that they are very, very stupid, I would think that they remember me singing '*The hills are alive with the sound of music*' to them last term.

I thought I'd go down to the river and look for the owlets there. I went to the little bridge, and I can see the path that leads up to Dother Hall. Underneath me is the Heck River. That Beverley threw herself in because of Cain.

Yes, there it is, the mighty Heck River, swollen to twice its depth by the incessant rain. So now it's four inches deep. What a fool that Beverley is. When she threw herself into the river, she just ruined her frock. The water only came up to her bottom.

I wonder what size her bottom is now after her hunger strike.

Anyway I'm not going to be intimidated by the Bottomley sisters this term. I am, after all, fifteen and not a kid who...

And that's when I saw them.

The Bottomley sisters.

Well, three of them – Beverley wasn't with them.

Ecclesiastica, Diligence and Chastity were eating pies. In fact, Chastity had one in each hand. And it wasn't even lunchtime. They were eating pre-lunch pies.

And I bet they're having pies for lunch.

When Eccles saw me she said, "Oooh, look, it's the long dunderwhelp."

Chas said, with her mouth full, "My mum said she saw you, sitting on blind people on her bus."

Dil said, "Come on, let's go, she's putting me off me pie."

And they went past me, eating and giving me the evils.

Eccles turned back and said, "Oh, I forgot, our

Beverley told me to give you this. So here you are, you lanky idiot."

And she gave me a grubby bit of paper.

As they lumbered off, Ruby and Matilda came tumbling along. Ruby was out of breath. And Matilda had to have a little lie-down.

"I saw you. I drew me curtains, I was up in my room and I thought, ay up, there'll be trouble. So we came to your rescue. What did the big daft lasses say?"

"They gave me a note from Beverley."

Ruby said, "Can she write? Is it a death threat? Give us a look."

She took the note from me and read it slowly, tutting, and then she said, "That Beverley can't really do joined-up writing, but I think it says, 'To the lanky streak of lard'."

What?

Ruby said, "That's you, Tallulah."

"What is?"

"You are the lanky streak of lard."

"What's lard?"

"It's fat made from bits of cow."

Nice.

She went on. "Then it says, 'If tha knows what's good for thee tha'll shut it and sling yer 'ook.'"

I looked at her as if she was speaking rubbish.

Which she was.

She explained, "Erm, well, in a nutshell it says, 'Shut up and clear off.'"

Charming.

There was more. Ruby read out, "'He's not interested in a bumberskite like you, it's only because tha threw your sen at 'im and gallivant around like a tit.'"

"When have I ever done that? I don't even know how to gallivant, let alone like a... and what is a bumberskite?"

Ruby had really got into it now. She went on.

"Yes, he, that's Cain, isn't interested in a bumberskite like you. Cain's not interested in you because you're like a sort of bum in a skirt."

"Thank you, Ruby."

"And secondly, because you threw yourself at him."

I started going red. This was so awful.

"Threw myself at him? Threw myself at him!!!"

I was getting redder than red, this was a nightmare come true, then Mr Barraclough shouted from the pub, "Ay up, Ruby, it's nearly dinnertime. Stop prattling with that big lad – next thing you know you'll be wearing his clown shoes."

Ruby started pulling on Matilda's lead. "I'd better go before he sees his socks that Matilda ate."

Ruby and Matilda tore off towards The Blind Pig.

I looked at the note. I suppose it's like a threatening letter. I've never had one of those before.

What does Beverley know?

She can't know about the thing that even I have forgotten about.

Can she?

Anyway, I'm not going to be blackmailed by the Bottomleys.

I've got my own little gang. The Tree Sisters.

Wait till I tell them about the note.

Except that I can't tell them about the note because then I'd have to tell them about the thing that I can't remember.

And that even if I could remember I wouldn't mention it to myself. I'll keep the letter from Beverley as evidence, in case of an unexpected pie attack by the Bottomleys.

To cheer myself up after the horrid letter, I thought I'd go back and get my Darkly Demanding Damson Diary from its secret hiding place, and look at my ideas and notes from last term.

I calmed down a bit as I looked over all the notes I'd made. Here are my poems and short stories. Ooooh, I'd forgotten about writing *The Daughter of Fang*.

And here are some sketches for my dance tribute to *Withering Tights*.

Oh, teehee, here's a sketch of Dr Lightowler.

In the name of Baby Jesus's nostrils, she has got ENORMOUS glasses on. Perched on the end of her beak. I don't know why she's taken against me so much. Ho hummity hum.

I'll put Beverley's letter in my secret hiding place right at the back.

Oooh – here's the James Bond book that Dad gave me. He said, "Best you learn the real facts of life" and I had read it last term, and re-enacted a corker-holding scene ♥ and Cain saw me through my window and... but I won't think about that.

Talking of corkers, Cousin Georgia said she could certainly see signs of life in my T-shirt when I ran for the bus. And in fact, as a celebration, she bought me a special packet of crisps that are actually called 'Corkers'. It said on the packet, 'Hand-cooked in sunflower oil, we're sure you agree that Corkers are another great British tradition in the making.'

I've got Georgia's Ace Gang 'snogging scale' in here somewhere. ♥ ♥

♥ See corker-holding with winter socks scene in the back of this book

♥ ♥ Don't look in the back of this book. Oh go on then.

I've stuck it in on a page right in the middle of my diary underneath a picture of the Dalai Lama. Although the Ace Gang's snogging scale doesn't really fit with mine, so far. I've written mine on the next page.

It's called 'Lullah's Lulu-luuuve List'.

This is it:

1. Hand resting
(A friend of my brother's put his hand on my bottom at the bus stop and when I said 'what are you doing?', he said his hand was tired and he was resting it.)

2. Corker-holder release
(On the bus, the same boy undid my corker holder. And I had to sit there jiggling about, as the tissues that I'd put in it for extra corker-ness worked their way into my armpits.)

3. Bat kiss
(Floppy Ben from Woolfe Academy kissed me after we went to see 'Night of the Vampire Bats' and tried to put

his tongue in my mouth. And it felt like a bit in the film when a bat was trapped in someone's mouth, just barging around.)

4. Nose-licking
(Cain licked a hailstone off my nose. I can't discuss this.)

5. Proper kiss possibly lasting two minutes, with additional praise for knees
(Boy (Charlie) kissed me really nicely so that I felt wobbly and he also said he liked my knees.)

6. Cain Hinchcliff came up unexpectedly on the moorland path and he... and he... ooooh, proper kiss, lip nibbling and tongues
(Oh Holy Mother of God, bless me for I have sinned. With the Dark Black Crow of Heckmondwhite.)

CHAPTER 3
Return of the lunatic twins

*I*t was already dark when the Dobbins came back.

I was in my squirrel room and heard heavy breathing outside my door.

Dibdobs whispered, "Do you know who's in there, boys? Shall we knock on the door and see who answers it?"

One of the twins said, "Eth."

There was knocking near the bottom of my door. I got up and opened it.

The lunatic twins were in their fun-fur hats in the shape of otter heads. And sucking on their dodies. They looked at me and then both grabbed me round the knees and put their heads into my legs. Dibdobs was almost crying at the beauty of it all.

"Ooooh, boys, it's Lullah, she's come home!!!"

Max (or Sam) looked up and said, "Ug oo."

And put his head back in my leg.

Then Sam (or Max) looked up and said, "Ug oo."

And put his head back down.

Then Max (or Sam) said, "Ug oo."

This could have gone on for years.

Dibdobs took charge.

"Right, boys, split splot, let's get your jimmy-jams on and then have our tea with..."

They looked up and said, "Ug oo."

And put their heads back into my legs.

We managed to prise them off at last and half an hour later Dibdobs called me down to tea.

The boys were in their jimjams now. Still with

their otter hats on.

They started shuffling towards me for more knee–hugging, but Dibdobs stepped in firmly and said, "Let Lullah sit down, boys, and have her supper. Lullah, it's a local supper."

Max said, "Bogie supper."

Dibdobs ignored him although she went a bit red. "The eggs are from Jessica and Maureen. Maureen's the one with the club foot."

I was just thinking I don't know any woman with a club foot when I realised she meant Maureen the chicken.

As I ate my supper, the boys stood about an inch away from me, looking at me and sucking. It was very unnerving. They certainly do not get any less odd.

Dibdobs was prattling on.

"So much going on, Tallulah!! I must tell you about..."

At that point Max fell over Micky the tortoise.

Dibdobs laughed and said, "You silly old chap, Max, you just fell over Micky on to your bottom!!!"

The lunatic twins rocked with laughter. It was like being in the House of the Mad.

Max said out of the side of his dodie, "An' sjuuuge bumbums. Look at my bumbums!!!!"

And he pulled down his pyjama bottoms.

Sam started laughing so much I thought he would choke. And both the boys began yelling, "Bum bum bum bum!"

Dibdobs said, with a fixed smile, "Yes, it is funny, boys, but pull up your jimmies now, that's enough. You're BIG boys now, aren't you, and..."

Then they both started rubbing their bottoms together and shouting, "Bummity bum bum."

Dibdobs lost her rag and flicked at them with her tea towel. "Boys, boys, that's not funny."

I quickly finished off Maureen's egg and stood up. "Well, that was a lovely supper... I think I'll turn in now, just do a bit more creative thinking for tomorrow. Night-night."

As I went up the wooden stairs, I heard Harold come in. The boys were still squealing and Dibdobs yelled, "Now what will your father say???"

Harold's voice rumbled up as I opened my bedroom door. "Put your bottoms away, boys. I've got some live maggots in my pocket."

When I got into my bed, I flicked through my Darkly Demanding Damson Diary to look at my Lulu-Luuuve List again, and it fell open at the last page.

There was the poem that Cain had pinned to the tree with a knife.

Written in thick untidy writing.

Like he'd got a twig and dipped it in ink.

Love looks not with the eyes, but with the mind
And therefore is winged Cupid painted blind.

And underneath:

I know tha likes this sort of thing
See thee later.

Did it mean he knew I'd liked kissing him?

Did he even know we'd got to Number 6 on my Lulu-Luuuve List?

No, he couldn't know that because I've just made it up.

I could do with some proper girl company. Thank goodness I'll see the Tree Sisters tomorrow.

Hurray!! The Tree Sisters together again. Vaisey, Flossie, Jo and me. We used to be five, but Honey, dear lovely Honey, has gone to Hollywood. She's been, what do you call it? Talent-spotted by an American entrepreneur.

Hey, I've just thought of what you'd call it if the owlets had been spotted by an American entrepreneur looking for talent in the bird world.

Talon-spotted!!!!

They'd be talon-spotted!

I'm going to write that down in my diary.

I may turn out to be a comedy genius.

CHAPTER 4
Snogs ahoy!

On Monday morning, I struggled against the wind walking over the bridge to Dother Hall. I'm early so I'll go and stash my stuff in my locker then find the Tree Sisters. If Bob hasn't burned the lockers as fuel. I hope the money thing is better than it was last term. Or at least we've still got a roof. I dread to think what would have happened if Honey's manager hadn't come up trumps with cash to keep Dother Hall going.

I miss Honey. She is sooo Honeyish.

And knows such a lot about boys.

Maybe she'll come back and visit. Or we could visit her!

Yarooo, I feel like a real performing artist. I am one of an elite gang of 'entertainers' our sole purpose in life is to give give give of ourselves.

My only worry is that I'm not sure I've anything to give.

The rest of the Tree Sisters have special talents. Vaisey can sing and dance and act and Jo can sing and act and Flossie can sing and act and she's really great at art. And Honey is *so* good at everything that she's been taken to Hollywood to be in films, and then there's me.

Ms Fox ("Just call me Fox. Blaise Fox") our dance tutor believes in me. She thinks I have my own very special quality. Well, what she actually said was "Watching you perform is like watching someone set fire to their own pants. Strangely riveting."

So that's good, isn't it?

Isn't it?

Dr Lightowler has hated me ever since I accidentally flew off my bicycle and destroyed the backstage area during my Sugar Plum Bikey ballet. Oh and because I did spontaneous Irish dancing in her class. When we were doing a tragic improvisation of the Brontë sisters dying of consumption.

And maybe because I pretend she actually IS an owl.

But this term I'm going to show her and everyone else that I am Tallulah Casey, superstar in the making. Bleeding feet at the ready.

Walking along the woodland path I passed the sign 'Woolfe Academy for Boys'.

That's where Charlie goes.

Oh, Charlie. I hope I can be friends with him. The last thing he said to me was, "See you next term, gorgeous." And he said I was a really good kisser.

It's just that he's got a girlfriend.

I can be grown up though. You know, so what if he's got a girlfriend?

Girls and boys can be mates.

We can be mates.

I might even be mates with his girlfriend. That's how matey I can be.

I don't mind tiny people. I like them.

I turned the next corner and saw Dother Hall. With its towering ramparts and cock-eyed spiralling chimneys. High up on the roof, if it wasn't sleeting, you could see all the way to Grimbottom. And past the woods to the grey brick walls and mullioned windows of Woolfe Academy.

The place where naughty boys were sent. Bad boys like our friends Charlie, Phil, Jack and Ben.

Naughty boys who are watched over by a stern and strict one-legged headmaster.

A man that Charlie says demands and gets their full respect.

A man that he and Phil call 'Hoppy'.

Which reminds me, Phil, Jo's boyfriend, is officially back. After serving his time at Woolfe, he was sent off to ordinary school. But it was a short stay because he dug a secret tunnel under the rugby pitch. He was going to unexpectedly pop his head up during a match for a laugh. But sadly the tunnel collapsed and the rugby squad fell into the hole.

Phil had done it for Jo. He said freedom was nothing to him if she wasn't there, punching him on the arm and shouting at him.

I wish someone felt like that about me.

I wonder if they ever will.

They won't get a chance if the Bottomleys get to me first.

As soon as I walked through the gates, Jo came running out of the front door. All little and shiny and dark, jumping up and down like a mad terrier, shouting, "Loopy Lullah!!!!"

She gave me the usual dead arm. Violence is her way of showing affection.

She was followed by Flossie, who has such a

long fringe that her face really only begins at her glasses. For some reason she often finds herself (in her mind) in Texas.

Flossie was in Texas now.

I knew because she was walking really slowly and fanning her face like it was a thousand degrees, and drawling in a Deep South accent, "Why, Miss Lullabelle, I do declare, it's too goddam hot. I was axing and axing, 'Where in the name of hominy grits is Miss Lullabelle?' And here y'all are!"

Vaisey was at the back, dear Vaisey, with her curls bouncing and her little bottom... er... bouncing as well. She came running to me and threw her arms round me. "Oh, Lulles, Lulles, I've missed you."

And we had our first official Tree Sisters hug. It was so good to be with my pals again. Nothing can go wrong when you have your little girl gang around you. Nothing!!!!

Back in the Theatre of Dreams with my gang!!!!

I started singing *"There's no business like show business, we smile when we are down..."*

And doing high skipping. I don't know why,

but my legs got excited.

A voice behind me said, "I might have known. Tallulah Casey. WALK properly, you are not a silly baby."

Oh, how I remembered that voice. I didn't have to turn round to see who it was. I could feel beaky eyes staring into the back of me.

Dr Lightowler.

Half woman, half owl, half really, really horrible to me.

Well this term she was going to see a big change in me. She wasn't dealing with a little kid any more. I had grown and not only in the corker department.

Vaisey whispered, "Don't say anything to annoy her."

I stopped and turned round. Blimey, I must say, and this didn't seem possible, Dr Lightowler looked even more owly. Had she got a new winter cloak?

She glared down her thin nose unblinkingly. I smiled cordially, my legs together.

"Ah, Dr Lightowler how marvellous to see you again. You look rested. The rest has done you good. In fact, you look in beak condition." (Oh sweet Jesus!) "Er. Hahaha, woopity doodah... peak, PEAK condition."

The girls were snuffling and putting their heads down to hide their laughter.

Dr Lightowler wasn't laughing. She was looking and not blinking. She hissed, "It's a shame that the rest of us aren't as impressed with you as you are, Tallulah Casey. Remember, I am watching you. And I don't like what I see."

And she swished off.

Flossie said, "I think deep down, really deep down, so deep down that she'd have to get a rope and the emergency services to get there, she's very, very fond of you."

Vaisey put her arm round me. "It's so unfair, just because you fell off a bike once she never gives you a chance."

How right she is.

Jo was jumping up and down. "Oh, shhhh,

shhhhh. Don't let's start talking about Lullah. I want to snog Phil. He phoned me and said he'd be at our Special Tree!!! So snogs ahoy!!!!"

As we walked into the main hall, Vaisey said shyly, "I got a postcard from Jack. I think he might like me."

I gave her a hug. "Who doesn't like you, missy?"

Flossie said, "Fiddle-de-dee, I just want to see some menfolk. LOTS of menfolk. ANY menfolk. It's this goddam relentless heat."

I didn't point out that there was ice on the inside of the windows.

The main hall was full of babbling girls. Milly and Tilly, Honsy, Bibby. It was nice to see everyone again. Groovy to see the 'showbiz' crowd.

I was leaning against the stage, queuing up when a posh voice said, "Oh, Tallulah, begorrah, bejesus. Did you have a noice time in your holidays?"

It was Lavinia and her mates, Davinia and Anoushka.

Lav, Dav and Noos.

For some reason, Lavinia pretends she's Irish like me and treats me like I'm a half-witted five-year-old. I can't really *not* like her because she's so 'nice' to me. But it's only because I know Alex and she rates him.

In fact, as I was thinking that, she said, "We must see that friend of yours again. What was his name... Alex? When he next comes home, to be sure, to be sure."

She swished her copper hair as she went off.

Flossie said, "SHE loves you as well. There's a lot of love in the room for you, Tallulah."

Gudrun, Sidone's assistant, came onstage with the register. She was covered in knitwear from top to toe, including a knitted beret. Flossie said, "Is she a knitted person?"

Gudrun shouted at us, "*Achtung, Fräuleins!!! Bitte!! Achtung! Ve mussen* sign the register!!!" (She always gets a bit German when she's left in charge, it goes to her head.)

We carried on chatting. Gudrun shouted again, "*Wilkommen*, girls. *Danke* for your attention. Erm, those girls at the back, will you just come down from the stag's head? It's an heirloom and not for sitting on. I don't know how you got up there in the first place, and we don't want any accidents..."

At that moment the stag's head and the girls on it crashed to the floor. We all cheered.

After registration, we went to the loos. It was freezing in there. And when I went to use one of the taps it fell off in my hand. There were no towels, just a notice written by Bob:

No paper towels this term – we are saving the rainforest, dudes.
Remember,
Be a shaker
Not an endangered resource taker.

I had to dry my hands on my leggings.

As we came out, Bob was dragging a big roll of plastic sheeting up the stairs that led to the roof. I said, "Hi, Bob, didn't recognise you without your horns."

He said, "Yeah, it's a bummer because my first love is the band, but hey, you've got to earn your bread."

Flossie said, "What's the plastic sheeting for?"

Bob said, "There's been, like, a roof incident."

Jo said, "What incident?"

Bob said, as he huffed and puffed away, "Well, dudes, it's essentially blown off."

I said to the Tree Sisters, "Get your umbrellas out, you're going to need them when you go to bed."

The rest of the morning we had tutorials and sorted out rehearsal times and class syllabuses and book lists, so we didn't see much of each other until lunchtime. Still no sign of Sidone. Apparently, she's doing some community-work thing.

Jo said, "She thinks the community will try to help keep Dother Hall going."

We laughed.

At lunchtime bell, we all met in the café. Vaisey

is mad keen to go to the Special Tree to see Jack and Jo looks like her head has exploded she is soooo excited about seeing Phil.

Flossie said, "I just want to see some boys. Any boys. Let's go let's go let's go!!!!"

After a bit of lip gloss and hair shaking and a reviving lunch on the run (Cheesy Wotsits), the Tree Sisters were ready to face the boys of Woolfe Academy.

Well, most of us were.

I felt shy about seeing Charlie again. I know he said he was sorry and had handled the whole snogging-me-but-having-a-girlfriend thing badly. And he'd said, "You're top, Tallulah and don't let anyone tell you any different." But that sort of implies that other people WILL tell you different, doesn't it?

If you say "Don't let them tell you", that means they might tell you.

And that... oh, I don't know.

And also, should I ask about his girlfriend? Like a mate would.

Do I ask politely if she's still tiny?

Hang on, is that my dream or has he actually said she's tiny?

I mustn't say she's tiny if she isn't tiny because that would be... tiny-ist.

No one noticed I wasn't as keen as they were.

Vaisey and Jo were doing very fast walking, crunching through the leaves and bracken to get to Phil and Jack.

Flossie said to me, "So do you think about those Hinchcliff boys, Miss Lullabelle?"

Uh-oh.

I said, "No, I don't. They're wild, uncontrollable animals."

Flossie said, "I know, that's why I like them so much. I'd like to see that Seth boy again. I wonder where he is."

I stumped on and said, "In a cave somewhere, I should think. Or prison."

We reached our secret place, our secret meeting

place in the forest. Where we danced around our Special Tree.

The Special Tree where Honey told us we should be proud of every part of ourselves. Flossie's glasses, Jo's conker hair, Vaisey's wiggly bottom, even my knees! Yes, even my knees!

A chill breeze rustled the leaves left on the trees, there were no signs of life. No birds or creatures and certainly no boys.

After five minutes of kicking leaves and hunching her shoulders against the cold, Jo said, "Where are they? Phil promised he'd come to see me on our first day back."

I was sort of disappointed and relieved at the same time. I said, "Well, they're not here so…"

Vaisey shouted from behind the tree, "Do sausages grow on trees?"

Flossie said, "Vaisey, is this like 'why did the sausage cross the road?' because I'm not interested in sausages, I'm interested in boys. If you'd said 'do boys grow on trees' you would have got my attention. But the sausage thing – no."

That's when we saw what Vaisey meant. Attached to the back of our Special Tree was a sausage with a ribbon round it and underneath it, an envelope.

Jo grabbed the envelope and ripped it open. Then started jumping up and down saying, "Ohohohoh!"

I said, "What? What? WHAT?!!!"

Jo's face had gone all pink. Flossie put a hand on her shoulder to hold her down. Jo panted, "It's from Phil. It's his writing. He sent me lots of photos of himself over the holidays. In unusual poses."

Vaisey started to say, "What sort of unusual..." until I shook my head at her.

Jo was in full flow reading out the sausage letter.

"*Dear Tree Sisters,*

Yes, I do mean you, Vaisey, Jo, Lullah and Flossie, this letter is from us. The lads. The top lads of all time. The bad lads. The lads... sorry, I had to stop there because Charlie got me in a headlock until I stopped writing 'lads'. What's he like? He's such a lad... sorry, another break there, he did it again. Anyway, we can't be with you because we are on a special bonding workshop all day with no breaks.

Hoppy says it will give us an identity as a group and respect for others. Mostly it's press-ups and stabbing sacks with sticks."

Flossie said, "Cor."
Jo continued.

"I know for a fact you like that sort of thing, you naughty girls. Anyway, we can't get away till tomorrow so I crept out and left this note and a sausage in case you were peckish.

See you tomorrow.
Phil, Charlie, Jack and Ben.
PS Big snog, Jo, you tiger (that's me Phil by the way) xx
PPS Charlie here. Hi everybody x
PPPS Cheers, Vaisey, Jack x
PPPPS Hi, everyone and Flossie, very much looking

forward to seeing you again. Ben x"

As we walked back to Dother Hall, Jo was jumping around in front of us, telling us about the photos that Phil had sent.

"There was this one of him with a human-sized inflatable banana he'd taken shopping. He bought it some shoes in a shoe shop and..."

Flossie had learned to juggle in the holidays. She said, "I think you'll find it very entertaining."

I made the mistake of saying, "I don't really know how juggling can be – erm – entertaining."

Flossie put her arm round me, which was a bit alarming. She said, "I'll illustrate for you, my little chum, how very, VERY entertaining juggling is. Everyone give me your tights."

I said, "No way, I'm not going to take my tights off – it's bloody freezing."

Vaisey and Jo both said no, they wouldn't either.

Five minutes later, Flossie showed us how she could make our tights into little juggling balls. She juggled our three tights balls with one hand

and threw her tights ball up in the air from behind her back. She was doing four-tights ball juggling. After she bowed, we clapped and quickly put our tights back on.

She said, "You see? Do you? How Very Entertaining that was?"

Vaisey said, "Oooooh, I tell you what I did in the holidays, I learned to play the guitar and I used my lucky plectrum that Jack gave me. If The Jones play any gigs soon, maybe I could jam along."

I could imagine what the Hinchcliffs would say to a girl 'jamming along' to one of their songs. I laughed and said, "Yeah, you could 'jam' that one Cain wrote especially for Beverley Bottomley when he dumped her, *Put your coat on, girl, you're leaving* and the follow-up when he dumped her again, *Is it so very wrong to want you dead?*"

Jo said, "What's happened about the Cain thing – is he still on the run, Lullah?"

I went a bit red and quickly said, "I've no idea. With a bit of luck Mrs Bottomley will shoot him."

Flossie said, "Oh, you are sooooo unreasonable,

Miss Lullah. Yes, those boys are BAAADDD, but they are so goddam handsome."

I said huffily, "Yeah, if you like Dark Black... animals in trousers."

Flossie said, "I do, as it happens."

Vaisey was trying to be nice. "P'raps they're just a bit misunderstood."

I snorted. "Vaisey, do you remember that Cain got Jack to dump you because no girlfriends were allowed in The Jones? He said it was a band rule."

Vaisey blushed.

Flossie sashayed about. "I am looking forward to seeing that bad Seth Hinchcliff again, oh and Bat boy. He's not quite so floppy since Honey gave him the snogging lesson."

I said, "You're insatiable."

Flossie said, "I know, but remember what Honey said about boys: 'alwayth have one ow two on the go. Theth thafety in numbeth.'"

We walked along, thinking about lovely golden Honey in her new golden life in Hollywood. Then Flossie said, "What about you, Miss Tallulah, what did you get up to in your holidays?"

"Well, I was staying with Cousin Georgia and she told me how to do sticky eyes and showed me her snogging scale. It's from one to ten." ♥

Jo said, "Yeah so, are we going to use your cousin's snogging scale?"

I said, "Well, it doesn't really fit with my Lulu-Luuuve List so..."

They all looked at me.

Jo said, "What's your Lulu-Luuuve List then?"

I wanted to tell them about it but not all of it, so I said, "Er, well, I've written it down and I was going to bring it in... but I forgot because I got a threatening letter!"

Flossie said, "What? From someone who thinks you should keep your Lulu-Luuuve List to yourself?"

"No, honestly, a real threatening letter saying I was like a bum in a skirt and if I knew what was good for me I would clear off."

Jo said, "Was it from Dr Lightowler?"

♥ Go on. Have another look.

I went red. "No, it was from... from Beverley Bottomley. She said I gallivant around like a tit."

Flossie said, "Well, she does have a point, Lullah."

Just then Gudrun came out of the front door of Dother Hall, wildly tinging her hand bell, and shouted, "Go straight to your classes, girls, Ms Beaver has double-booked herself with the Blubberhouses Large Ladies Who Pole Dance For Fun Society, but she will definitely be in to welcome you at some stage today."

Thankfully, I'd got away with the Lulu-Luuuve List thing for now.

But then Jo said quietly to me as we went in, "Did your Cousin Georgia tell you what number 'nose-licking' was on her snogging scale? Is Cain licking your nose on your list?"

She's like an elephant in a dress.

How on earth could I tell them that nose-licking was quite literally the tip of the... er, the tip of the... nose on the face of the snogging Cain list?

I know I should tell the Tree Sisters everything, and I will.

Soon.

CHAPTER 5

The Blubberhouses Large Ladies Who Pole Dance For Fun Society

*M*onty was our tutor for the afternoon. He bustled in. "Hello, hello, girls!!! Happy days!!! *Le* Show RE-commence!!!"

He was wearing a tartan suit and pink waistcoat. The waistcoat was hanging on round his tummy for dear life. Just by one button.

He went to sit down on his chair but then paused and took to standing and leaning against his desk. I suspect the spirit was willing to sit down, but the suit wasn't.

He was beyond himself with enthusiasm. His chubby hands clapped together in delight.

"Girls, I am THRILLED, absolutely thrilled about the project this term. Shakespeare's *The Taming of the Shrew*, the Bard's masterpiece about the battle of the sexes. Of course this is often misunderstood as a battle between a man and a woman.

"For the more artistic and creative soul like myself it can of course be interpreted as the battle between our masculine and feminine parts. As a man, I, of course, have a delicate female part hidden. And you girls have a secret male part hidden in a secret place."

Flossie said, "Is he saying I have a goddam man lurking about in my dance tights?"

Jo said, "You might have. Monty definitely looks like he's got more than one person in his suit."

And we began laughing uncontrollably. It didn't matter though because Monty was off in

Italy with his mates.

"I first saw *The Shrew* as a young man in a nightclub production in Italy. Ah, gilded youth! Biffo and Sprogsy, my great pals, were with me. It was our first trip abroad and we didn't know it was an all-male production. The boy in the part of Kate was most convincing. The Italians are much more at ease with finding their Inner Woman."

Monty got us to discuss what we thought 'Being a Woman' meant.

Flossie said, "Well, ah don't rightly know if ah could say, sir, maybe ah could show you…" And she started her Southern belle routine, sashaying around the room.

Monty clapped his pudgy hands. "Marvellous, marvellous, Flossie. I know, girls, let's go with physical expression to feel our way into the mood. Let's pursue Flossie's idea of being a spoilt Southern belle! I'll start."

At the very last bell, Sidone burst into the classroom.

She was a vision in fur.

Well, she was in fur.

I don't know what kind of animal is purple.

She leaned against the door, panting.

Monty flung his arms wide. "Girls, girls, here we have it, before us, Woman!!!"

Sidone blew kisses to us all individually which went on for quite a long time, then said, "So sorry, my dears, not to be here to welcome you back, but the Blubberhouses ladies were very demanding. Such big, big women. The poles will have to be replaced of course.

"Anyway, I wanted to be here to welcome you, but such is life. In order to keep Dother Hall going sometimes I must rent my services out to amateur groups. I do it willingly, of course, but the headaches are quite violent afterwards. But... what do I matter??? It is you, my dears, who are the hope for the future. I am just a dim light from the past, blinking in the firmament of you bright little starlets."

Monty leapt in. "Nay, nay, madam, you remain

the brightest light, the brightest!"

Sidone tinkled with laughter and shook her head at him. "Too kind. And yet perhaps I still have some of the old skills."

She suddenly did a high kick which only just missed Monty's chin. He was ecstatic and clapped like a seal in a suit.

I noticed Sidone was holding her leg as she said, "Girls, here are your instructions for tonight, your FIRST night of many first nights, if you will excuse the theatrical pun."

Which we did because we had no idea what she was talking about.

She handed us each an envelope.

"Open it this evening and bring your ideas for Ms Fox tomorrow. Till then, my dears, my dearie dears." Kissing her hands, she withdrew from the room.

I said to Flossie, "Did you think she was limping slightly as she went out?"

We were all tired at the end of the day. The Tree

Sisters gave me a hug and went off for supper and a lie-down. Flossie said, "If Bob hasn't burned our beds for firewood."

I wish I could just have my dinner and pop upstairs instead of trailing all the way into the village. Even though the Dobbins are nice.

When I got to the village I kept my eyes peeled for the Bottomleys, but they weren't around. I saw Ruby bundled up in her coat on the doorstep of The Blind Pig with Matilda. They both looked glum.

I said, "What's up, Rubes?"

She said, "Me dad went spare, we have to stay out of his sight. I can't have any tea and when he's had his, I have to go straight to bed. All because Matilda chewed his Viking helmet. She thought it was a hoofy snack."

I said, "That's bad, little pal."

I sat down beside her and Matilda put her sad, crumpled-up face on my knee.

"Maybe we could go and have a proper look for little Lullah and..."

Then I heard Mr Barraclough shouting, "Look at the state of this!!! One of my horns is a stump."

I thought I'd better nip off.

Eccles and Dil were sitting on the church wall. Stuffing crisps into their mouths and looking at me.

Ecclesiastica yelled out, "Are you not gone yet, lanky loser?"

And Dil said, "Yeah, we're watching you."

And she did that pointing at her eyes and then pointing her fingers at me.

Charming.

In the kitchen of Dandelion Cottage, Dibdobs had her head in a cupboard.

I said, "Hello."

And she said from the cupboard, "Hello, Lullah. Nature has many treasures we can use to beautify our lives. At no cost at all!!! Look at this. I've attached some copper wire to these and..."

She came out of the cupboard with fir cones dangling from her ears, smiling in an enormously smiley way. She said, "Fir-cone earrings!!! Paint them with a bit of silver and *voilà!* I don't think I'd feel out of place at the palace!!"

The twins came out of the cupboard.

I managed to get to my room by first of all saying how marvellous the twins' new leaf hats were and then that I had homework to do.

I lay down on my squirrel bed and tucked a squirrel slipper beside me. I'm going to do my homework. Right, I'm opening the envelope from Sidone.

Girls, my girls,

Start to explore your feelings through Art and Theatre. Get used to tapping into your Inner You-ness. The You that makes you you-nique. Access your feelings and bring them to the surface.

How do we do this? How do we share this inner world with our audience?

Well, some examples:

Are you happy? Happy to be back at Dother Hall?

Feeling full of creative juices? Of course you are. Why not experiment with coloured scarves or tambourines.

Or maybe you are angry? Frustrated by a world which is disinterested in art and artists. I myself often do an expressive stamping dance. To let my feelings free. I growl or shake my hair about angrily. You may feel like swishing your hair about. You need accompaniment. Choose an unusual instrument to pluck.

A comb perhaps?

And so on.

That's the bit, isn't it?

The 'and so on' bit. That's when you're on your own.

Right, I'm going to express what I am feeling.

What am I feeling?

The wind is whining in the trees. I'm sitting in bed with a squirrel slipper and little Lullah and little Ruby have left me.

I'm feeling lonely. Yeah, lonely.

Lone-lee.

So how shall I express that physically?

I'll stand up and slouch around in a lonely way. Slouch slouch. Yeah.

Yeah, dragging my feet, good.

Sighing.

But I'm also feeling angry. Angry that Dr Lightowler hates me for no reason. Angry that the owls have left me. Angry that the Bottomleys have sent me a threatening letter.

Anger-ee.

Saying it out loud is quite good.

"Lone-lee."

"Anger-ee."

It's got a rhythm to it. Maybe I could do a sort of rap song. About anger and loneliness but...

But the twist is – the words are about owlets, but it's really about Dr Lightowler and the Bottomleys. I'm not going to think too much. I'm going to pace about and bang stuff like rappers do.

Right, I'm pacing.

Up to the door, back to the window, up to the door, back to the...

Ow. I've just banged my toe on the bed leg.

It's making me quite angry actually. Because I can only do about four paces before I bump into something wooden.

I want to hit something.

I'm going to hit something. I'm banging a squirrel slipper on the dressing table. Yeah! It feels good.

Right, I'm pacing, pacing and banging the slipper on the bed end. Now on the wardrobe door. Yeah yeah!! I'm stepping up the rhythm now, pacing and banging anything I pass. Pace, pace, bang, bang.

Bang the window sill.

Bang the door.

Bang the bedhead.

Bang the lamp... oh damn... pick up the lamp.

It's about owlets leaving and not even bothering to say goodbye after all I've done for them. Here we go:

Oh yeah
Everything leaves

Oh yes uh
(bang bang)
Without warning
Oh yes uh
(bang bang)
Squeaks from a beak
Crunch in a cheek
Mouse gone
Owl gone
Oh yes uh
(bang bang)
Everything goes
Oh yes uh
(bang bang)
Without warning
Not even in the morning
Rastafari
Uh.

I wrote it down quickly in my Darkly Demanding Damson Diary. It looks quite cool. But why have I turned into a Rastafarian at the end?

It was swishing my hair around that did it. I think I was imagining dreadlocks. Maybe that's what Monty means about finding your Inner Maleness.

Maybe I have an Inner Rastafarian Bloke.

I think Blaise will get my rap though. At least she likes me. Well, she thinks I'm unusual.

The wind had gathered, the temperature had dropped and it felt like snow was on its way. Brrr.

I put my feet on the hot-water bottle that Dibdobs brought me. It's got a knitted jacket on it. Harold made it at his men's knitting circle. And I do mean a jacket. With a collar and buttons.

I bet Harold will be able to help me a lot with *The Taming of the Shrew* – he's constantly talking about his Inner Woman.

Then something thudded against my window. Maybe it's a branch blown off by the wind. Or... no...

It had better not be Cain up to his old tricks!

I flung back my curtains and opened a window

to the chill night air. There on the window sill was little Lullah!

Or maybe Ruby?

No, it was defo little Lullah because her legs were so long and gangly.

I felt tears prick my eyes as I looked at her. Her owly yellow eyes were staring and blinking back at me. Oh, oh, she'd come to see me!! Because she loves me. I hope she didn't hear the rap song.

I said, "Little Lullah, it's me, your big owly friend. You remember me; I give you nice mice snacks."

She raised her lower eyelids and fluffed out her feathers. "Woooooo."

I felt so proud. She was wooing at me.

I said, "Wooo to youuuuu tooo. I didn't mean it about the rap song, it was about other owlets, not you." And I went to kiss the top of her head.

It must have startled her to see a big head coming towards her because she fell straight off the window sill backwards into the garden.

I peered down into the gloom. My God, had I killed my offspring? But then I saw her flutter upwards. And immediately crash into the dustbin. She took off again and this time went straight into the garden shed. Finally she swooped off into the woods. I could see her bobbing up and down and crashing to the ground until it was too dark to see her any more.

I shivered and shut the window. At least an owlet loves me. In its owly way.

Or perhaps she thinks I'm the Big Owl in the Sky and have some dead mice to give her. To be honest, she must be starving by now if her flying skills are anything to go by. The mice probably just sit in little mouse deckchairs, watching her hopelessly swooping around, crashing into things.

I felt even more guilty about the rap song now.

CHAPTER 6
Boy Ambush

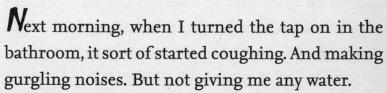

*N*ext morning, when I turned the tap on in the bathroom, it sort of started coughing. And making gurgling noises. But not giving me any water.

Dibdobs was passing the bathroom door with a lunatic twin under each arm. She looked harassed, but still smiling. "Morning, Lullah dear. I'm afraid the water has frozen in the pipes so we're going to fill a bath in front of the fire downstairs, aren't we, boys?"

Sam said from upside down, "Wiv Micky."

Dibdobs said, still laughing, "Well, no, Sam, tortoises don't like baths."

Max joined in. "Dicky is liking barf, lady."

Dibdobs was getting a bit stern, the end of her nose had gone red. She gripped the boys more firmly round the pyjama-bottom area and said, "Now then, hippity skippity bobbit, off to the bath!"

Both of the twins said, "Wiv the Mickys!"

As she struggled off down the stairs, the twins were quacking loudly.

Do they think tortoises quack? Perhaps tortoises do. I've never heard one, but they might do it in their shell in their private time.

I went back to my room and Harold popped his head round the door.

"Well, good morning, Tallulah. I've brought you some hot water in a jug and an old basin that you can use to scoop it over yourself. I've used the same method at my Iron Man group when we went on our excursion to Scunthorpe. Marvellous simple times. In the evenings we sang round the fire and did a bit of knitting. That's when I knitted your hot-water bottle jacket. You see, there is a vast untapped well of womanliness inside every man." He went away, chuckling to himself.

It was freezing in Dother Hall. The Tree Sisters looked very bulky, because they had most of their clothes on. I said, "Wow, are you that cold?"

Flossie said, "Let's just say that I've got two pairs of pyjamas on underneath my joggers and top. We all have. The roof is a piece of tarpaulin."

Vaisey said, "The clingfilm on the dorm windows doesn't keep the wind out."

Jo said, "My head has gone numb."

Gudrun was wearing a coat made out of hamster skins. Or maybe mice.

We went into the dance studio first thing. I hadn't seen anything of Blaise Fox so far. It would be nice to see her. We've got her twice today.

Jo said, "I'm not taking anything off for dance

class, and anyway I can't move my legs."

Blaise Fox strode in, wearing a ski suit, yelling, "Good morning, sensation seekers. This afternoon you'll show me your works of genius but for now let's go for the burn!!! I've got my big drum, let's get moving!!!"

To warm up we had to be horses. Trotting round the hall. Then light cantering. The drum got quicker as we did galloping, slower as we did 'dressage' then back to banging and pauses as we did galloping again. For the horse finale we did the Grand National and Blaise shouted "And OVER the hedge!!!" leaping.

Then we did the Grand National again as different animals. Blaise shouted out, "Cows!! Run run LEAP over the hedge. Moooooo-ve, girls. Hahahahahaha! Now then, it's the ferrets! Scamper scamper scamper and OVER the hedge!!"

Flossie pretended her ferret couldn't get over the hedge and had fainted. Blaise shouted, "Come on, you ferrets, help your furry pal over the hedge!!"

So we had to gather round and try and pick up Flossie. And try to get her over the imaginary hedge. It certainly made us warm.

Finally, as the bell rang and we were almost on our knees with exhaustion, Blaise shouted, "Last round... stroppy teenagers. Leaping over the hedge!!!"

So we all ended up stamping about, refusing to get over the hedge and storming around complaining that it wasn't fair. Blaise said we were "terrifyingly lifelike".

Jo turned into a madwoman at lunchtime. She was yelling, "Come on, come on, stop tarting around! Let's get to the tree." Pushing us out of the loos quite violently.

Vaisey said to me, "Gosh, I'm excited about seeing the boys. Are you excited about seeing them? Well, especially Charlie, Lullah?"

I said, "Yeah, it'll be nice to see him, because he's, er, a nice mate, isn't he?"

Vaisey said, "I think he's more than nice, I think he's yummy. Do you think he's yummy? Do you think about Charlie? Did you think about him in the holidays? You like him better than Batboy, don't you? He says quite funny things to you, doesn't he? He said 'Praise the knees'."

And she started giggling and waggling her curls about.

She was right; he pretends he's a knee worshipper, it makes me feel quite nice.

We trudged along through the woods in the cold. As we passed the big oak tree, Jo said, "I'm going to be quite stand-offish with Phil at first to teach him a lesson. He was the one who got himself sent back to ordinary school for being too good and that split us up. I think a cool approach will teach him some respect and..."

Phil crashed down on to Jo from a branch above us. They rolled and shrieked around. Then out from behind another tree popped Jack and Ben.

It was a boy ambush. Vaisey went bright red when she saw Jack and waved at him. He waved back.

Flossie put her hands on her hips and shouted in her Southern belle way, "Mr Goddam Jack and Mr Goddam Ben. Why, I do declare, you were hiding yourselves away behind that tree and you so goddam handsome and all!"

Where does she get all this stuff from?

Jo yelled from underneath Phil, "Group hug! Group hug!"

Flossie dived on to my back and I fell on top of Phil, and who knows what was happening above me. I couldn't breathe because of Flossie and I couldn't see anything. Ben's voice said, "Hello, Flossie, like, really nice to see you. You know?"

I brushed Flossie's hair out of my face and another voice said, "Aha, I see the woodland games have begun, let us in!!!"

It was Charlie! I felt an uuumph as he dived on top of us. He shouted from above me, "Aha!!! We are back and this time we are NOT serious!!! Yee-ha!!!"

After a couple of minutes of having all the breath in my body squeezed out of me, Jo shouted, "Get off, my head is popping!!"

We untangled and I tried to pull bits of hair out of my mouth. Flossie pulled me on to a log and yelled, "Log time!!!"

Charlie sat next to me and smiled. I smiled back but looked away quickly. I was almost shaking and felt my face going red.

Phil pulled Jo on to his knee and said, "Come here, little Miss Dynamite Nutcase," and started jogging her up and down like a little horsey. He was saying, "A joggity-joggity-jog."

She said, "Phil, stop jogging me up and down otherwise I will have to hurt you!"

"...a joggity-joggity-joggity..."

Jo started wrestling with Phil which turned into snogging and they fell off the log. Flossie went over to Ben who was staring at her, but I stayed still. So did Charlie.

So then I couldn't get up because it would look like I'd noticed that I was sitting next to him.

Charlie said to me, "It's nice to see young people enjoy themselves, isn't it, Lullah?"

Flossie had Ben pinned against a tree trunk and was making him try her glasses on. Charlie said, "He looks terrified but sort of pleased."

I said, "That's the kind of effect that Flossie has on people."

Charlie said, "I've got snacks." And he offered me a crisp.

Sitting next to him and chewing was making me so tense I could feel my legs twitching. Was I chewing too loudly?

I'll do really gentle, quiet chewing. That's it. Slight chew, no crunching, pause and...

At this rate it was going to take me a week to get through one cheese and onion crisp. I should say something normal to Charlie about a show I'd seen or something. Yes. That's the ticket. A show.

I haven't seen any shows.

Jack and Vaisey were humming little tunes together and now and again Jack would drum with sticks on a tree and Vaisey would nod along.

It was quite a good rhythm...

No!!! I am not doing alfresco Irish dancing and that is a fact. So before my legs got any funny ideas I blurted out to Charlie, "Did you have fun in your holidays?"

Then I thought, *Oh no, he'll think I'm asking about his girlfriend.*

So before he could think that I went on. "I did. I had great fun. I had loads of laughs, loads. In fact, I pretty much didn't stop laughing all holiday. I stayed with my Cousin Georgia and she's a laugh, such a laugh, and then her Ace Gang came round and we had, you know, a..."

Charlie said, "Laugh?"

And he smiled at me.

A proper light-up-your-whole-face smile.

He said, "Tallulah, I meant what I said last term about thinking you're a really great girl and—" And then the others came and pushed us off the log in a surprise attack.

As we left our Special Tree to go back to Dother

Hall, Phil gave Jo a big smackeroonee on the lips and said, "*Au revoir*, you little cracker, I'll see YOU later."

Jo said, "No. YOU won't see me later because YOU are going back to the Bad Boys' School and YOU will have to go to your beddy-byes because you are so baaaad. And A Disgrace to the Nation."

Phil stood nose to nose with Jo. "That, my little mad missus, is where you are very, very wrong, because I will be a-sneaking out of my bedroom window and a-sneaking into your dorm tonight."

He kissed her again and turned away with the other boys. He shouted as they went off into the woods, "So be warned, girls, Big Phil is coming a-calling tonight! *Arrivederci*."

As we scuffed along, Jo said, "He won't really come, will he?"

Flossie said, "No, he's not that much of a fool."

Jo looked at her and Flossie said, "Is he?"

CHAPTER 7
You don't want to do any more winking back

I felt quite chuffed. Charlie has more or less said he likes me. Well, to be factual, he'd said I was "great".

As we went into the studio, I said to the Tree Sisters, "Now I get the chance to show my rap to the world. I hope Blaise likes it. It's her kind of thing."

At which point, Mrs Fox came out, putting her crash helmet on. She said, "Hello, groovers, just

off to rescue Sidone from the weightlift[...]
class in the Scout Hall. It's a mission of merc[...]

As she was passing, I said, "Oh, so are you...
shall we do it later?"

She stopped and said, "Do you want to do it later?"

I was a bit confused but I said, "Er, well, yeah."

Blaise said, "Well, that's good then, isn't it? Go
ahead."

She went off and we heard her bike roar into
life. Oh well. I'm a bit disappointed not to be
doing my rap now but... that's when I saw Dr
Lightowler come into the studio.

She said to us, "I'm taking over Ms Fox's class.
Prepare to show me the homework that the
headmistress set you."

Oh no! *Will Dr Lightowler guess that my rap is
about her?*

She's very sensitive to owly issues.

Maybe I should say that I'd left it at home.

As I thought that she swivelled her head
towards me and said, "You have done your
homework, haven't you, Tallulah? Or didn't you

think it applied to you?"

It's almost like she has extra-sensory hearing through her eyes.

I said, "No, I have done it."

She looked at me through her glasses and said, "No, I have done it...?"

I said again. "No, I have done it, Dr Lightowler."

I could feel my cheeks burning. Vaisey squeezed my hand. Flossie looked cross-eyed at me and Jo did a secret throat-cutting sign.

Vaisey went first and sang a song she'd written about love and music. It was called *Song for Jack* and she played her own tune on guitar. Dr Lightowler said her guitar playing showed promise.

Tilly did a quite dramatic dance about escaping to the circus. She ended by doing the splits. Dr Lightowler said it was "accomplished and athletic".

Flossie sang, "*Take me back to the Black Hills, the Black Hills of Dakota, to the beautiful Indian country that I love.*" She had a little whip that she cracked.

Dr Lightowler asked her what emotion she was

revealing and Flossie said very seriously, "Well, Dr Lightowler, I know you've travelled extensively in the Southern States of America. You know the longing for freedom. The heat and the passion, the young men cooped up in the—"

Dr Lightowler said, "Yes, yes Flossie, I do understand. Again, beautifully sung, your voice is very strong. You've obviously been tuning your instrument. Well done."

Then Dr Lightowler said, "Now I think we're ready for you, Tallulah Casey. What delights do you have to show us? Is it the usual Irish dancing?"

I said, "No, erm, well, it's a rap."

Dr Lightowler looked at me. Then she winked. She closed one eye anyway. Maybe she thought that was what rappers did.

Maybe they did.

So I winked back.

I heard an intake of breath from the Tree Sisters.

Dr Lightowler said, "What on earth do you think you are doing?"

I said, "Well, I winked at you."

She said, "Why?"

I felt how a mouse does just before a big owl gobbles up its head. Was she literally going to bite my head off?

I said, "Er... it's part of the rap... performance."

She shook herself and said through clenched teeth, "And what is your 'rap' about, Tallulah Casey?"

I said in a small voice, "Well, it's about anger and loneliness, but expressed in a... in a..."

Dr Lightowler twitched her head. "In a WHAT?"

I said, "Well, in an owly way."

Again I heard an intake of breath from the girls. Dr Lightowler looked like her glasses were going to steam up.

I did my rap. I put my heart and soul into it and used everything in the room to do the beat, hitting the walls and the desks even turning the light switch on and off.

When I finished, the girls applauded wildly.

Dr Lightowler said, "Stay behind at the end of class."

Dr Lightowler paced up and down while I stood there. Finally she said, "What makes you think you are so special?"

I stammered, "Well, I don't, I don't think that. I love owls and I was..."

She came and stood really near me and bent down to look into my eyes. "I know your game and I will not stand for it. Do you hear me?"

I had no idea what she was talking about, but also I didn't want her to bite my head off so I just thought nodding was the safest thing. As I nodded, she winked at me again.

Spooky dooky.

The Tree Sisters were all agog when I came out. I said to them, "She did wink at me, didn't she?"

Flossie said, "It's hard to tell, but you definitely don't want to do any more winking back."

Next we had a *The Taming of the Shrew* talk with Monty. I still feel shaky. Dr Lightowler really does seem to hate me.

Monty told us that it's Kate who is the shrew. I thought a shrew was a little furry creature with twinkly eyes, but Monty explained that a shrew can be a rude description of a bad-tempered woman.

Everyone laughed, but I bet some of them didn't know. Or maybe they all did. That's the trouble with me never having gone to theatre school.

Monty said, "Kate is a headstrong, independent woman with a sharp tongue and a quick temper. She refuses to listen to her father when he tells her how to be nice to men. In the end, Petruchio bets that he can get Kate to be nice to him. He's going to 'Tame the Shrew', do you see???"

I said yes, but actually I don't think Kate is a shrew just because she doesn't want to be bossed around by blokes. Fair enough, I think.

It's a pity there's nothing in the play about being bossed about by owly people.

At home in my squirrel room. Boy, what a day.

On the one hand it was lovely to see Charlie

and he had said nice things to me. But then Dr Lightowler raised her beak again. She really does think I do things to annoy her. And, well, I suppose I do a bit.

But I won't any more, she's too scary.

That night I had a vivid dream.

I was in a hedgerow with some sheep. It was dark but I fancied a worm. *Hang on a minute*, I thought (in my dream), *Why do I fancy a worm so much?*

And also, by the way, why am I in a hedgerow?

A giant owl landed in the hedge and winked at me with one of its huge goggly eyes. I said, "What are you winking at, Beaky?"

And it said, "I'm winking at you, Tallooooooolah."

I said, "Why are you winking at me? Haven't you got anything better to do?"

And the owl said, "I'm winking at you because I'm going to eat you."

I said, "Why would you do that?"

The owl said, "Because I can. Because it's a laugh. I call it, *The Taming of the Shrew*."

The owl handed me a mirror.

I looked in it and saw I had dark beady eyes and a pointy nose.

And I realised I was holding the mirror with four claws.

I was a shrew.

CHAPTER 8
The fire escape of desire

When I got to Dother Hall on Thursday, there was no sign of the Tree Sisters.

Normally they're bounding around, waiting for me.

The bell went for assembly. They still hadn't turned up, so I sat next to Tilly and said, "Have you seen the Tree Sisters this morning?"

She said, "No, but there was some kerfuffle in their dorm last night; we heard shouting and crashing. We were going to go and see what had happened, but Dr Lightowler shouted at us to go back to bed."

What was going on?

Then Dr Lightowler came on to the stage. I slumped down in my seat. Even for her she looked very owly. Were the Tree Sisters in some sort of trouble?

Dr Lightowler began in her thin, rasping voice. "You girls want to be treated like adults striving to make good in a career that is one of the most difficult in the world. We, the staff, work night and day to help you, even though in some cases it is a pointless task." And she looked directly my way.

Everyone looked at me. My whole head went red. Some of the girls giggled, but most looked a bit sad.

Dr Lightowler went on. "You all know how near we came to closure last term, and how much our future depends on our good reputation with our neighbours. Which is why last night's incident is so disgraceful."

What incident?

Everybody started whispering.

Dr Lightowler said, "Shh! I happened to be checking the building at lights out last night and heard laughter from the dorms. As I entered, unexpectedly A BOY..."

The whole assembly gasped.

Dr Lightowler went on. "...a boy fled out of the window and down the fire escape. He fell through the potting-shed roof and escaped into the night. APPARENTLY, none of the girls had ANY IDEA who this boy was. He had just 'appeared' and then leapt out through the window. One of the girls said she thought he was one of Bob's friends who had left by the wrong exit."

We looked at Bob.

Bob came clinking up to the centre of the stage. He had so many spanners on his belt that his trousers were practically round his ankles. "Listen up, dudes. My buddies do not leave through windows. They never have, they never will. That is our code. It is also a health and safety issue: a window is not a door. End of. This is like bad news."

Dr Lightowler said, "Thank you, Bob. I..."

But Bob hadn't finished. "Secondly, this is a major downer. The roof of the potting shed is like totally gone. I will have to personally gaffer in another twenty bin liners. That's a good twelve quid's worth. Think about it. Peace."

He nodded and started to leave the stage and then said, "Oh and just put your ears back on for a mo, dudes. The Iron Pies are doing a gig at Blubberhouses on the twentieth and it will be like mega so get your dancing boots on and come."

When we filed out of the main hall, I saw the Tree Sisters coming out of Sidone's lair.

I said, "What happened???"

Jo was livid. "I can't believe this. There was a scrabbling noise and he came in through the window."

I said, "Oh my goodness, it was Phil! Oh Our

Lady of Lourdes and Her Miraculous Tears, he actually came. Phil actually came into the dorm."

Jo was going on. "It's so unfair. Phil was just doing his Tarzan impression on the window sill and we were laughing when Owly burst in so he leapt through the potting-shed roof."

Vaisey said, "You can still see the boy shape."

Jo was going on. "And now I'll never see him again."

I said, "I think you will. I don't think that they'll kill him. Will they? It's not that bad."

Flossie said, "Well, it's all right for you to be philosophical, Miss Tallulah, but it's not you cooped up in this goddam steamy house. In the middle of the hot season."

Vaisey said, "I was hoping to go plectrum shopping with Jack at the weekend."

It turns out the Tree Sisters and the rest of their dorm are confined to Dother Hall until someone owns up about who knew the boy.

I put my arms round them in a spontaneous Tree Sisters hug. As we hugged, a couple of the other girls from their dorm came by and gave Jo the thumbs-up. After they'd gone, Jo said, "Look, this is ridiculous. He's my stupid boyfriend, you lot shouldn't have to suffer, I'll tell that it was Phil and..."

The Tree Sisters shook their heads.

Vaisey said, "We're all in this together and anyway it could have been Jack who came through the window."

Flossie said, "Yes or Charlie or Ben..."

Then, after a little pause, she said, "Well, maybe not Ben. He's too floppy to climb that far."

I didn't see much of the Tree Sisters during the rest of the day because they had to do extra background reading over the breaks. They're not even allowed to go out at lunchtime until further notice.

Jo whispered to me at the start of lunch, "It's down to you, Lullah. You have to go to our Special Tree and see if there's any news."

I said, "Oh well, you know, it's a bit sleety and cold and anyway..."

Jo gave me her maddest look. "See you when you get back. Wrap up warm."

Oh holy moly.

I got togged up and slipped out of the side door. Brrrr.

I am a truly great pal. If Dr Lightowler caught sight of me, she'd clap me in irons. Or expel me. She's just waiting for me to do something wrong after the winking incident.

I sneaked round the side of Dother Hall and scampered into the woods.

No one was going to be there on a day like this anyway.

It was freaky deaky, silent and cold and spooky. I crunched along to the Special Tree. Brrrrrr shiver shiver.

No one there, just as I thought. So I can go back now and unfreeze my bottom.

But then Charlie came crunching into the

clearing. Oh my goodness!

He smiled when he saw me and put his hands in his pockets. Gosh, he was nice-looking. He said, "Hello."

I looked down. He was making me feel very red and shy. And for the first time in ages I felt my knees looming about trying to say hello all by themselves. I pulled down my skirt and said, "Hello."

"Nice to see you, Tallulah. All by yourself?"

"Yeah, well, because of the, erm... potting-shed incident."

He said seriously, "Ah yes."

"The Tree Sisters are in detention, all their dorm is."

Charlie said, "Yep. Phil got caught coming into Woolfe Academy late so he's mostly in chains. We've had the Hoppy lecture on letting your friends down, letting your school down, but mostly letting yourself down. Have you?"

I nodded.

Charlie said, "Makes you feel dirty and ashamed

and yet somehow really feel like a Jazzle. Do you want one?"

I said, "Oooh yes."

As we sucked on our Jazzles, he said, "How are the owlets?"

I said, sucking quietly and being casual, "Well, you know, a bit... a bit..."

"Owly?"

I said, "Yes, yes, owly. Well, I think so. They've flown the nest, but they're useless at flying so how will they catch anything? When I tried to kiss little Lullah's head, she fell off the window sill backwards. Ruby said that the mice laugh at them so I might have to, you know..."

He said, "What?"

"Er... make them snacks... to tide them over."

Charlie said, "Snacks?"

Oh God. I'd said I was going to make snacks for owlets. I must say something to let him know I am not completely insane. My dream popped unexpectedly into my head so I said, "Yes. Er, shrew snacks."

Charlie said, "Nice." And then he laughed. But in a good way.

He's got a lovely laugh. It's deep and warm. Like he thinks I'm funny. I laughed too. He's got nice crinkly eyes.

His hair's a bit longer. It suits him.

I looked down to think of something to say and noticed that the front of my coat is sticking out. In the corker area.

Oh no, I wonder if he's noticed that my corkers have grown. It's the kind of thing that Cain would notice.

But I don't want Charlie to think I am deliberately thrusting my corkers at him.

You know, in a girl way. In a 'ooooh, look at my corkers' way.

I'll hunch my shoulders a bit so that the sticking out is counterbalanced by my hunching. Not too much though. I don't want him to think I've become a hunchback over the holidays.

Charlie was looking at me. What should I say to make the situation more normal and matey?

What do boys say to each other?

You know, to their mates, erm...

I said, "Everything all right at home?"

Charlie grinned even more. "Yes, thanks. All well at your end?"

I nodded. "Yes, erm, tickety-boo, thank you."

Tickety-boo?

Then Charlie said, "Look, it's really nice talking to you about, you know, 'home' and everything, but it's all a bit prison break at Woolfe because of the Phil incident so I should go back."

I said, "Yes, yes, sorry to hold you up, it's just that Jo wanted, you know, to know if Phil is all right."

Charlie said, "I've got a note from the villain himself." And he handed it to me.

I said, "Oh, she'll be so happy. Thank you."

Charlie turned to go. "It's lovely to see you again, Lullah... and, well, I hope I'll see you a lot more. Bye." And he gave me a hug.

I flapped my arms against his back. And then gave him a thumbs-up.

I don't know why.

Maybe I am a man.

Jo was ecstatic to get her note. She read it and said, "I'd tell you what it says, but it's very personal and private."

We all nodded and were going off when she said, "Oh, go on then, you *are* my besties. Here's a bit of what it says, I won't go into the snogging stuff...

"Jo, you little wild love bucket, you know I had to climb the fire escape of desire to see you. But then as you also know I sadly fell through the potting shed of life and slightly bent my l—"

Then Jo started giggling uncontrollably and said, "No, no, I can't tell you that bit, but this is the last thing...

"I'm confined to my room and under constant

surveillance. I won't go into what they're doing to me, but it was worth it to see you."

I thought Jo was going to burst into tears.

She said, "I'm going to hide it under my mattress in case I'm strip-searched in tap class this afternoon."

I said, "Jo, we are free theatrical spirits. This is not a prison camp. We're not little kids any more. We can't just be bossed about by—"

Dr Lightowler came by and shouted, "If you've got a spare moment to waste gossiping, you need to be running around the school. Into your PE kit, girls, and ten times round the garden walls."

As she went, Jo said, "Yeah, good point well made, Lullah."

On the way back to the village after college, I was walking fast. The woods were rattling with cold breezes and there were odd calls and hoots. Maybe Connie the owlets' mum was out there looking for some supper for them. It looked stormy and clouds flitted across the darkening sky. I cuddled into my coat and thought about the day. Wow, plenty of boy action one way or another.

Before I came to Dother Hall I hadn't had much to do with boys and now I knew a little group of them. It was really exciting to be part of everything.

Like Cousin Georgia. She had her Ace Gang and I have my Tree Sisters. The only difference is that out of all of them, I'm the only one who hasn't got a boyfriend. I know Flossie hasn't officially got a boyfriend, but she could have Seth or Ben. Or both probably.

It's nice being friends with Charlie, but he still gives me a shaky, excited feeling in my knees.

And tummy.

And heart.

Also my hands feel a bit shaky when he's around.

And my mouth.

That's a lot of shaking. And I don't think

shakiness is really a friendy thing.

And then there's Cain. Lurking about, being absent.

It's very tense-making, waiting for him to pop up. And he's always popping up when you least want a person to pop up. Like when you're adjusting your corker holder. Or doing a bit of corker-measuring. Or rubbing your corkers with hiking socks to make them grow. That's when he pops up.

And the most popping up of all the popping things he's done was on the night when he popped up on the back path. And snogged me.

But that is something that will remain locked in my Darkly Demanding Damson Diary forever. He can do what he likes as far as I'm concerned.

I reached the bridge. The famous (not) drowning bridge. Where Beverley Bottomley jumped off to drown herself. Because Cain was supposed to be going out with her and she turned up at a gig to meet him and he was snogging another girl. So now she's starving herself to death.

She must really like him.

But why?

He's so horrible to her.

He's horrible to me.

He's always sort of mocking me because I don't know about stuff. But after all that, he goes and kisses me. And writes a poem to me. Even though it looks like it had been written by someone with hoofs instead of hands.

Perhaps he has got hoofs and not hands?

Have I actually seen his hands?

Maybe he's the Devil.

Oh Holy Mother of God. That's why he's got hoofs instead of hands!

I'm being silly now – how could he play the guitar with hoofs?

Hang on.

He doesn't play the guitar.

The Blind Pig was all lit up as I walked across the bridge and Ruby and Matilda came skipping along to meet me. Ooooh, it was so nice to see them.

Ruby shouted, "There she is, Matilda. There's big Loopy Lullah with her legs!!! Go seek!!"

Matilda came charging to meet me, but slipped on some stones and started to slither down the riverbank. She was just looking back at us as she slowly slipped down the bank. With big blinky eyes. Occasionally, she'd look forward and see the river approaching and then she'd look back again. For some reason it made me laugh so much I thought I might pee.

Once I'd pulled myself together I went and got her out of the river and I kissed her on the head. I wished I hadn't actually because she smelled really horrible.

Ruby said, "Dun't kiss her – oh, too late. I've just rubbed her down with a cod skin – it's good for her fur."

I was nearly sick. Matilda looked miserable as

she squelched along beside us, her mouth was turned down. I said, "Oh, Matilda's bottom lip is all droopy. I think she feels like a fool."

Ruby looked at her. "She is a fool."

And Ruby tucked Matilda's bottom lip in and pulled her top lip over her teeth and said, "There, that's nicer now, she's smiling!"

I told Ruby about the Tree Sisters not being allowed out and about seeing Charlie in the woods.

She said, "Ooooh, Charlie. I like that Charlie. He's my favourite. He's reight good-looking. He's so hot he's like 'ouch ouchy'."

How does Ruby know about these things?

She said, "If you don't go out with him, I will."

I said, "Ruby, you're eleven."

Ruby kicked at a leaf. "I like older boys. So do you, you like Alex."

I stammered, "No I don't, well, only you know like a..."

Ruby said, "Like a div? Well, he's coming home the weekend after next so get over it!"

I started spluttering about not knowing what she was talking about, but then I heard Mr Barraclough behind me saying loudly, "Now, Ruby, I've told thee before, stop messing about with them lanky village lads."

And he shouted to me as I went off, "Be told, young man, she's too bloody good for thee."

Oh, here we go. I turned back and said, "It's me, Mr Barraclough, Tallulah."

And he put his glasses on and looked more closely.

"Bloody hell, well, I go to the bottom of our garden, it's you! I do apologise. My heartfelt apologies. It's just that in this light, well, it's a mistake that anyone could make. Is it a clown workshop you've had today? Thank goodness taxpayers' money is not going to waste. You're not being a clown now, are you? Are you still wearing the comedy shoes?"

And he went cackling off into the pub.

He loves it.

He loves having us to mock at Dother Hall.

I got out my Darkly Demanding Damson Diary when I got into my squirrel room and looked at my Lullah's Lulu-Luuuve List.

I wonder if I will ever get to Number 5 with a boy again.

Oh and here's Cain's silly poem.

I'll tear it up.

No, I won't. I might save it to use in a performance sometime.

Oh and here's the letter I wrote to Alex the Good last term and never posted.

Dear Alex,

It was really nice to see you last weekend and to talk about theatre. I love the theatre, it's great, isn't it? I think if I could just be on the stage all the time I would be truly happy. Not all the time, I mean I'd like to do other things. Like sleep and go shopping and so on. But apart from that do you...

I didn't get any further than that. Just as well I didn't send it to him because he would have probably read it out to his floaty girlfriend Candice.

How come I can't be like Candice?

All floaty.

I suppose I could get a floaty top from Skipley. I think I will.

CHAPTER 9
I've eaten snail shells

The Tree Sisters are not allowed out at the weekend.

At break on Friday, after a read-through of the banquet scene in *The Taming of the Shrew* with Dr Lightowler (who made me be the half-witted manservant), Flossie said, "If I don't get out of this goddam hellhole, Miss Lullah, well, I'm just gonna go plum crazee. I ache for the touch of a maaaan. Why, I even found mahself axing Bob if he'd thought about growing a li'l moustache cos I thought it would suit him real fine."

This can't go on, somebody is going to snap. Jo keeps gazing at the boy-shaped hole in the potting-shed roof. She says it makes her feel nearer to Phil.

At the end of the day, Jo said, "I'm giving myself up to the Camp Commander. I can't stand it any more. Don't try and stop me."

When she said "Camp Commander", I thought she meant Monty, but she was talking about Sidone.

We persuaded her to wait it out. They can't keep the whole dorm cooped up forever.

Vaisey said, "Come on, Jo, how bad can things get? It's just staying in a bit, isn't it? We're not being tortured."

At which point, Dr Lightowler came beaking along. "You girls on remand, no TV tonight. Instead we are experimenting with living as the Brontës did. Go and see what you can find in the garden to cook for supper and then it's a magic lantern show."

Poor Tree Sisters.

Trudging home, I was thinking about tomorrow and Sunday. I haven't got anything to really look forward to. I'll be just on my owny.

I wish I could get Charlie to like me not just in a matey way.

Maybe I could try 'sticky eyes' like Cousin Georgia said?

She says you have to look at a boy, right in the eyes and then look down. Then you look at him in the eyes again. And then down again. Sort of like really slow blinking. I could try that with Charlie.

And Honey said if you believed you had 'inner glorwee' then everyone, especially boys, would think you had it too.

Maybe I should try 'sticky eyes' and 'inner glorwee'.

But how exactly do you find your 'inner glory'

when you need it?

I really, really miss Honey. She would know about all this.

Dibdobs had made me a boiley egg for tea. And the lunatic twins were at Little Foragers' Club so it was almost like a normal house. She said, "And I've made you soldiers, Lullah, with the bread that Harold baked."

As she said that, Harold came in, all togged up in bicycle gear. His helmet looks like it's got a grass rug on the top of it. He said, "This grass is a marvellous insulator, my head is quite snug. Sure you don't want to come on the snail hunt with me and the Little Foragers, Tallulah?"

I smiled and said no, sadly, I had homework to do.

Dibdobs beamed and said, "Aaaaaah."

Harold beamed at me as well.

They do a lot of beaming, the Dobbins. I

crunched away at my toast. Blimey, it was very crunchy. I said, with my mouth full, "Thith bread ith, well ith... lovlyth."

Harold said, "Aaah, having some of my bread, Tallulah? I've added ground-up snail shells to the mix. I think it gives it a special flavour and it's a tremendously good source of zinc."

I have eaten snail shells.

That is my glamorous theatrical life in a nutshell.

Well, a snail shell actually.

After they'd gone out, I was a bit bored so I decided to go through all my clothes and make-up. So that took ten minutes.

Then I tried a bit of the layering of mascara that Georgia told me about. Then I put my hair up like Lav does, sort of loosey-goosey, so that it slightly falls down. And I put on my new skinny jeans (the red ones).

I'm ready to go out, but I haven't got anywhere

to go out to.

Hmmm.

I went over to find Ruby and show her my new look. As I got nearer the pub, I could hear shouting coming from inside. And an occasional guitar riff. Oh, I'd forgotten The Iron Pies were rehearsing, they've got a gig soon.

It'd better not be too soon.

I poked my head round the front door into the main hallway and shouted up the stairs, "Hello, Ruby, are you around?"

There was no reply from upstairs, just loud drumming from the bar. And a guitar. The guitar kept starting and stopping. And I could hear Mr Barraclough swearing. Then I heard Bob's voice. "Dude, dude, listen up!!!! Listen to what I'm playing on the drum line. That is what you have to follow. The beat is der der der der – DER DER."

Ted Barraclough's distinctive voice shouted, "That's what I was doing."

Bob said, "No, dude, you were doing der der DER der DER der."

They tried it again, this time with more guitars, and then Ted shouted, "Lads, lads, leave it."

The banging and twanging came to a halt.

There was a little silence and I think a sigh and then Ted said slowly, "Bob, Bob, Bob me old son, can I just stop you there and ask you a little question?"

Bob said, "Cool, I'm always here to help."

Ted went on. "Whose band is this, Bob love?"

Bob paused.

"Well, I guess it's a... collective based on the talents of the whole of..."

Ted said, "Ah, I see, this is where you've got your sen mixed up. It's not a 'collective', old love, it's 'MY band'. Does tha see? Does tha see what I mean there, Bob?"

Bob said, "Yeah."

Ted said, "Reight, that's good, me old flower. So, from now on, you follow *me*. I will set the rhythm... Now then, the next song is the well-known Beatles song *All You Need is Pies*. Hit it, lads!!!"

And the banging and twanging and shouting

began again with Ted singing loudly, "*All you need is pies, LA LA LA LA, All you need is pies pies, pies is all you need!!*"

Ruby came in behind me with Matilda and shouted above the racket. "Ay up, I'm just going to take Matilda for her evening poo. I've finished with that gormless Joey – he crashed into my legs when he were riding his bike backwards."

She went off into the kitchen to get snacks and I was nuzzling Matilda. Although keeping away from her back end because of the imminent poo business. She was wagging her tail, well stump really, when a pair of trousers appeared before my eyes.

Not just any trousers, not magic trousers floating around in the air.

When I looked up. There he was.

Alex the Good.

He smiled at me. Phwoar. He was so good-looking, like a film star.

I couldn't think of anything to say.

What was he doing here? This wasn't the

weekend after next.

He shouted above The Iron Pies, "Tallulah!!!"

And he hugged me.

He smelled gorgeous, like a vanilla ice cream with everything else in it you like. Chocolate brownies, touch of raspberry sauce and, er chips.

No, not chips, but something that tasted like chips but didn't smell like them but...

He said, "Are you pleased to see me, lovely Lullah? Look at you, look at how you've grown."

My face felt beetroot. "My brother says I'm growing upwards to get away from my knees. But..."

Ruby came tumbling back with her arms full of crisps. She said to Alex, "Has she said anything weird yet?"

Alex smiled at me and said, "Nothing out of the ordinary. Come away from this racket and tell me what's been happening, Tallulah."

Ruby said, "I can tell you what she's been doing. She tried to kiss the owlet and it fell off the window sill and then..."

Matilda started whining and rubbing her bottom on the floor.

Alex said, "Ruby, you'd better take her out now." And Ruby went out of the door tutting and pulling Matilda by the collar. She said, "Don't talk about stuff that you don't tell me about."

Alex smiled at me and said, "Let's go outside, otherwise my dad'll see us and you know what that'll be like."

Oh yes, I knew what that would be like. I said, "He pretends I'm a long lanky village boy."

Alex laughed. "He would."

We strolled up the back path. I walked along like a dozy butterfly sucking in the nectar of his Alex-ness.

He said, "So then, what's been happening since I've been away?"

I said, "Er, I did a rap song about the owlets. "

He laughed.

I wanted to tell him everything so I said, "Beverley Bottomley is on hunger strike, she—"

Alex interrupted, "Yeah, I heard about Cain

being hunted down by Mrs Bottomley. He's a bloody idiot, that boy. He's always been in trouble, since his mum went. He was a right nice kiddie before then, wild and cheeky but nice. We used to go fishing and stuff together."

I said before I'd thought about it, "He's not that nice, he makes fun of me and does... er... stuff... and... now Beverley thinks... she said I throw myself at him, and it's not true, he started the licking thing and—"

Oh holy moly.

Alex stopped walking.

"He started the LICKING thing?"

I could feel redness creeping up my body.

"No, well, yes, but... no, it's not like that, well, a hailstone landed on my nose and he just licked it off like I was an ice cream. I told Cousin Georgia and it's not on her official snogging scale. Sooo."

Alex was looking at me intently. It made me very nervous and that was never a good thing. I found myself saying, "Georgia said she didn't know if it should come before or after lip nibbling but she didn't..."

Alex was still looking at me. "You seem to know a lot more about snogging than you did when I last spoke to you, Tallulah."

Now I really was red. How could I be talking to him like this?

Then he completely bamboozled me by saying, "He shouldn't have taken advantage of the er... hailstone. But you can't blame him for wanting to kiss you."

I could hardly speak but I tried. "Me? Kiss."

"Yeah, if you were a bit older, I might try to kiss you as well."

The whole of me wanted to yell, "WELL, JUST GO AHEAD, MATEY!!!"

Maybe this was my moment. I could say, "Well, don't let other people's silly rules get in the way. KISS ME, YOU FOOL and let me show you my inner glorwee."

But then Alex looked at his watch.

"Uh-oh, damn, gotta dash. I'm meeting Candice and the others in Leeds."

The Great world started rearranging itself into the Tallulah world.

I forced myself to smile.

"Oh yeah, I need to get a wiggle on. I'm off on, well, I'm, I should be going too."

Alex gave me another hug and said, "See you soon."

I am in my squirrel bed in a love daze. I must look at things factually.

In fact, I'm going to write the facts down in black and white in my Darkly Demanding Damson Diary.

The facts as I see them are:

1. *Alex the Good said that if I were a bit older he would snog me. (He actually said that. That is a fact.)*
2. *One day I will be older.*
3. *In fact I will be one day older tomorrow.*
4. *And two days older on Monday. In fact, I will pretty much be getting older all the time, every minute of the*

day. Unless the Bottomleys or Dr Lightowler kill me.

5. He said "See you soon". When he sees me 'soon', I will be older by however long 'soon' is.

So if we take Fact 1 (him saying he would snog me if I was older) with Fact 5 (I will be older soon), the conclusion is he has more or less said that he will snog me, soon.

That's how I see it.

But actually that is how a lunatic would see it. The actual facts are:

1. Even though it's seven-thirty I am going to bed.

2. I told Alex that I had my nose licked by Cain.

3. I can never let Alex see my nose again.

4. Therefore, I can never see Alex again.

On Sunday I lurked about hiding behind the trees next to The Blind Pig so I could check that Alex had left. But Ruby caught me at it on her way back from walking Matilda.

She said, "What are you doing?"

I said, "Er, I was thinking of making a... leaf fan for... the—"

She said, "He's gone back to college."

And went into the pub tutting.

Well, I can never see Alex again but at least I can let my nose run free.

In the afternoon, I was reading *The Taming of the Shrew*. It was a bit lonely in the cottage with everyone out. And there is a lot of "forsooth!" and "nay" and so on in *The Taming of the Shrew* and not so far, it has to be said, much snogging.

Oooh, I am so restless.

I could have gone foraging with the Dobbins or to see The Iron Pies play in Blubberhouses with Ruby, but I didn't feel in the mood. Normally I would have been larking about with my mates, but they're cooped up, being made to clean their dorm from top to bottom.

I needed to think about stuff in the fresh air. So

I decided to go hunting for the owlets again. Wow, the Alex thing has really unsettled me.

Even though it was so early, it was dark down the back path. The trees cut out a lot of daylight even without leaves. And it was damp and drear. The sheep saw me and tried to get in the hedge. How could they remember me singing *The Sound of Music* to them on that fateful day when Cain did his nose-licking thing?

Thank goodness he's not around.

He even spoils my life when he's not here.

Brrrr, it's cold and damp. I wouldn't like to be out on those black moors at night. Being shot at by Mrs Bottomley.

On the bright side, if she does shoot him, that would mean he couldn't tell anyone else about the snogging incident.

None of the Woolfe boys are around either. They have all been confined to barracks as well. It would be nice to have them, well, Charlie, for company looking for the owlets. He makes me laugh. And he doesn't make me feel so self-conscious about my knees or anything.

I wandered along the path, looking into the hedgerows for Lullah and Ruby. The path curved to the right and passed very close to the bus stop. Seth and Ruben Hinchcliff were lolling against the wall talking to three of the Bottomley sisters. I could see them but they couldn't see me.

There is a big family resemblance in the Hinchcliff boys. They are all dark and brooding looking. And handsome I suppose, if you like that dangerous wolf boy sort of look. Flossie will go wild when she finds out I've seen Seth in the flesh.

The Bottomleys have got a family resemblance as well. They are very big.

If I got a bit nearer, I might be able to hear what they were talking about. It was risky, but it could be worth it. I wonder if the girls are trying to get off with Seth and Ruben. That would be hilarious.

As I crept up, I heard Seth say, "For God's sake, play another bloody record, Eccles, give over mithering on about our Cain. Haven't you got owt else to talk about?"

Eccles said, "Well. My sister might die because of your brother. He's a bad un."

Chastity went on. "She still won't eat. She just lies there sobbing like her heart might brek. She's not touched a thing since he went except a small pot of Marmite a day."

Diligence said, "Not even on bread, just the Marmite."

Seth said, "Look, Dil, Eccles, Chas, be reasonable – Beverley is in no immediate danger."

Eccles said, "What, starving her sen to death?"

Seth said, "Well, she's safe for a good few months anyway just living off her fat bum."

Dil said, "You cheeky get."

The boys were laughing and Ruben said, "Well, you're all very well covered lasses, aren't you?"

Seth joined in. "Which can be a lovely thing to behold, girls."

Amazingly, the Bottomley sisters seemed to think that was all right.

Ruben said, "Any road, it's tha mother tha

should be talking to, she's the one with the bloody big gun."

The sisters turned to go, but then Eccles said something that made me shrink back into the shadows.

"It's all that daft long streak of lard's fault he's not around. Sniffing around him. Dressing up in daft clothes. Everything were awreet before they came. Them Dither Hall twits. Them bloody posh lah-di-dah madams. Tekin' our lads. Especially that Loopy Lullah or whitever she calls herself. Beverley says she went to find Cain and Loopy Lullah were there, pushing herself up to him reight close. Mekin' eyes at him. Fawning all over him."

The other two sisters nodded and Dil said, "And our Beverley wrote a letter to her. So she's had her warning. If she dun't clear off from our lads, she knows what she'll get."

Ruben said, "Oooooh, you didn't threaten to sit on her, did you, girls? That's bloody criminal that."

And he and Seth started laughing as the sisters evilled them and made off.

I felt a bit of a warm feeling towards the brothers even though they are awful. But I didn't like the 'Loopy Lullah' long streak of lard business. Being talked about behind your back was really not nice.

I was just about to creep off when Seth said, "Bloody hell, lasses are mad. Let's go and give Cain his tea and tell him latest news from the village of the damned."

Ruben said, "What's all that stuff abaht them lasses from Dither Hall? Some of em are reight fit. And what abaht thee with that big lass? Wot's her name?"

Seth spat.

Oh, charming.

"She's a bit of awreet, that Florence, just the right amount of meat on her and best of all she's not like these milky lasses round here. They get on me nerves, always moaning and saying, 'Ooooh, I love you, you're me boyfriend now you snogged me.' She's got a bloody hefty right hand as well.

But she's a cracking snogger and a good laugh. Ah might let her near me."

Ruben laughed.

I knew I should go away. But you know when you should go away because it'd be better all round if you did, but you don't?

Well, I was doing that.

Ruben said, "What's that daft Eccles going on abaht this lanky lass for? Loopy is she called? She's that one that looks a bit wild, black hair, green eyes with them lanky legs, isn't she? The one that sat on the blind bloke on the bus. Our Cain's not messing with her, is he?"

Seth said, "Mebbe. Ah dun't know. I wun't be surprised, he's not said owt but then he went out with your lass behind your back, didn't he? You know Cain, he can't leave lasses alone."

Ruben said, "Ah know. That's why he's got a mad woman with a gun after him. I wun't mind but we've got a Jones gig comin' up, he'll have to get it sorted."

They went off.

They say you should never eavesdrop because you might hear something you don't like. And I had. I'd heard that everyone knew I molested blind people. But worse, I'd heard that Cain can't leave girls alone. Not that I didn't know that because I did.

I'd been tainted by his nose-licking.

I wonder how many noses he'd licked in his life.

Bucketfuls, I bet.

I walked back along the path. Brrrr, it was dark and cold. Like Cain. Dark, cold and heartless. A heartless nose-licker.

But he was something else as well.

The thing I'd vowed never to remember again.

The thing that, no matter how much I try to forget, I remember.

That wild night up on the moorland path. When Cain had said to me, "Will you do summat for me? I want thee to kiss me."

And I had done.

He hadn't made me. I had wanted to.

The truth is... I'd liked it.

That was the most terrible thing.

Besides being a nose-licker and a rusty crow and an all round terrible human being... he was a great kisser.

I had kissed him back.

And I wanted to kiss him more.

CHAPTER 10
Snogging and Jazzles

On Monday morning, as I walked over the bridge to the woodland path. I heard loud gunshots from up on the moors. Surely Mrs Bottomley's not up there already?

Looking for Cain. I know everyone says she couldn't shoot a pig in a ginnel. Well, when I say everyone, I mean Ruby. But maybe Ruby's wrong, maybe Mrs Bottomley is really good at shooting pigs in ginnels. But I don't know what a ginnel is.

And why would the pig be in this ginnel, whatever it is?

I would ask Ruby, but she just looks at me like I'm a halfwit when I ask her to explain Yorkshire things. Anyway, I can't be bothered to worry about Cain. He certainly doesn't worry about me. It's beginning to be a pattern. Boys kiss me and then don't want to do it again.

Perhaps I'm not doing it right.

Maybe I should suggest to the Tree Sisters that we try snogging practice on the backs of each other's calves again.

Oh hang on a minute, last time it was horrific.

It was all right with Honey, she made it seem natural and sort of scientific. Saying helpful stuff like, "Yeth, good, onwy a bit thofter and not tho toothy." But when I did it on Flossie, she started her Southern belle thing, moaning and saying, "Oh, that is so goddam niiiiiiiice, Miss Lullabelle."

I wish Honey was still here. She used to make me feel good about myself. She thought I had oodles of 'inner glorwee' just waiting to burst out. I miss her.

You don't notice people not being around for a bit and then you think, "What's missing?"

And it's them.

Honey is so, so... Honeyish.

I bet she has loads of Hollywood boyfriends. Ones who say, "Have a nice day."

And what else do Hollywood boys say? Oh, I know. If you say anything at all, like... er... "Is your tea all right?" they say, "AWESOME."

Honey knows about boys.

She likes them.

Really.

As if they're normal people.

When I got to Dother Hall, the Tree Sisters were hanging around the door.

Vaisey said, "Oooh, Lullah, did you have a nice weekend? Tell us all about it, we were soooo bored."

I said, "Well, I ate some bread made out of snail shells."

Flossie said, "Er, was that the highlight?"

I said, "No, the highlight was—"

Just then the bell went and we had to go into assembly.

It's drumming workshop with Blaise first thing and I want to tell her about my rap.

I said to Flossie. "I think Blaise will appreciate my owl rap, unlike Dr Lightowler."

Flossie put her arm round me. "I don't think Dr Lightowler *didn't* like your rap – it's *you* she doesn't like."

Well, that gave me another lovely warm feeling.

Vaisey said, "Don't worry, Lulles, Dr Lightowler will forget about the winking thing."

Jo said, "Shhh about Lullah and her winking. I need to drum. I am really good at hitting things."

When we went into the hall there was no sign

of Ms Fox. Or any drums.

Gudrun came in wearing her knitted beret and said, "Rightio, girls. I'm afraid Ms Fox has stepped in for Ms Beaver who has a migraine."

Jo said, "Are you saying that Ms Fox is having Ms Beaver's headache for her?"

Gudrun laughed nervously.

"No, no, girls – Ms Fox has taken over at the Mature Woman's Skipping group in Little Waddle and I'm, well, I'm taking over for her! So let's begin, girls."

Jo said, "Where are the drums, Miss?"

Gudrun adjusted her beret and said, "Well, the thing is, there aren't any drums."

Gudrun beamed and clapped her hands. "As they say, 'necessity is the mother of invention' sooooo... we're going to have a CLAPPING workshop!!! Mittens off, girls!"

After what seemed like hours, the bell went. Jo was kicking stuff, doors and everything.

She said, "That was so boring. What is the point of spending an hour clapping?"

Vaisey said, "Well, I suppose it teaches you – er – co-ordination and teamwork."

Jo was still grumpy. "No. I'll tell you what it teaches you, it teaches you not to come to a college where there's a drumming workshop without any drums."

Vaisey tried to put her arm round Jo. "What's the matter?"

Jo said, "It's my fault that we're all cooped up here and made to run round the perimeter wall in our sports knickers."

Vaisey said, "Well, it's not really you, is it? I mean, it's more your boyfriend really."

Flossie said, "Who, to be frank, only came through our window to see you, so I suppose officially, not to put too fine a point on it. Yeah, it is your fault."

Jo was going on. "I've let the school down, I've let my parents down, I've let the Royal Shakespeare Company down, but most of all I've let myself down."

To cheer Jo up, I said, "Yes, that's true, but look, why don't I go to our tree today? If the boys turn up they'll tell me how Phil is."

Jo nodded miserably. "What if they've sent him away as punishment?"

I said, "Jo, he's already sent away as punishment. He's at Punishment Headquarters."

Jo said, "Anyway, it's not the same if you go. Why can't I go?"

Jo was impossible to be with for the rest of the morning. Kicking chairs and doors and sighing and moaning. At lunchtime she deliberately ripped down Bob's notice about paper towels and used it to dry her hands on.

Vaisey said, "I'll have to do something. I'm going to go and ask Sidone if we can go into the woods to practise an outdoor scene from *The Taming of the Shrew*."

Jo said, "Fat chance. What idiot would fall for that?"

Vaisey came back ten minutes later, curly and floppy and smiley. She said, "We're allowed!"

And we gave her the full Tree Sisters hug.

Jo said, "I'm not being biased, but I've always liked you best, Vaisey."

Vaisey went red and said, "Erm, we're allowed to go, but Sidone has phoned Hoppy and he says the culprit is under strict observation twenty-four hours a day and will not be allowed out."

Boo.

We got togged up in the loos and trundled off into the woods.

Jo was stomping along ahead of us.

"It's not fair! This is against my human rights. My boyfriend is being held prisoner in a free country. I may do a protest. I'm going to stop washing."

Flossie said, "Well, that would make Bob's day. I think he's got a master plan to make us stop using water altogether. I'm sure he says the loos are out of order on purpose."

Vaisey said, "Well, there was a vole blockage."

Flossie said, "Yeah, but have you thought how the vole got there in the first place? Did it have a vole ladder to get up the side of the loo?"

I couldn't help thinking that Flossie had a point.

Vaisey linked up with me and said, "I'm really missing Jack. Did you see anyone else at the weekend?"

Flossie said, "Yes, did you see any menfolk? Any handsome menfolk? What about those Hinchcliff boys?"

"Well, yes, I started to tell you before, I went down the back lane last night looking for the owlets..."

Flossie said, "Did you hear me say MENFOLK?"

I looked at her then went on. "And I heard Seth and Ruben talking to the Bottomleys by the bus stop."

Now I'd got her attention.

I said, "Yeah, the Bottomleys told them about Beverley's threatening letter. Seth and Ruben were quite funny about it actually. They said, 'Oooooh,

you didn't threaten to sit on her, did you, girls?'
And I laughed – inwardly – because obviously I
didn't want to be sat on. Anyway, the Bottomley
sisters said that us Dother Hall girls were posh
lah-di-dah madams. Taking their lads."

Flossie said, "So they do like us! Get to the
point about Seth. Did he say anything about me?"

I said, "Yes, he did, he's so full of himself –
they're all alike those Hinchcliffs. He said that you
were a 'bit of awreet' and you had 'a bloody hefty
right hand' and that you were 'a cracking snogger'
and he might let you be near him."

I thought she'd be furious but Flossie seemed
very pleased. She started swaying along, saying,
"Why, that Mr Seth, he dun talk real naaice."

As I was about to explain that, like all Hinchcliffs,
he was a creature from the dark lagoon we heard
an awful groaning and moaning. Like someone in
agony.

We all huddled together and tried to make
ourselves very small.

The groaning was coming nearer and there

was a crashing sound. Like something beastly was dragging itself towards us.

Then Phil crawled out of the undergrowth!!!

Dragging a ball and chain. Attached to his leg.

He looked up at us imploringly and said in a husky voice, "Jo, Jo, girls, girls, for pity's sake, save yourselves; the dogs will be on to me soon."

And he fell unconscious.

Jo rushed over. "Phil! My God, what have they done to you? It was only a potting shed." And she cradled his head on her lap.

Phil said weakly, "Hoppy. He did this. To keep me away from you."

Jo looked like she was going to cry. "Does it hurt anywhere?"

Phil said, "Yes, just here." And he weakly raised his hand to his mouth. As Jo bent to have a look, he snogged her.

What?

There was more crashing and Jack and Ben came running up. As they bent over, panting, Charlie jogged in. I felt myself going red so I put my head down.

Charlie said, "I think we've shaken them off, lads. Oh, hello, girls, what a lovely surprise!"

I sneaked a look up, Jo was still snogging Phil. For someone who couldn't walk he certainly seemed to have quite a lot of strength in his lips. Ben and Jack were smoothing their hair down and smiling. Vaisey had gone all red and couldn't look at Jack. Charlie gave me a wide smile and a thumbs-up.

Jo stopped snogging Phil and hit him on the arm. She shouted, "I've been really worried about you!!!"

Phil said, "I know but it's taken me over an hour to crawl here with this ball and chain. It's been hell."

Jo hugged him again.

I don't really think it's right to chain boys up, even if they are Phil.

Only Flossie was calm. She said, "Nice to see you, boys. You sure look all tuckered out. Fortunately I've got an emergency stash of Jazzles.

Anyone want one?"

Phil made a startling recovery by jumping to his feet, picking up his ball and chain and leaping over to Flossie. "Oh yeah, dreams do come true – snogging and Jazzles!"

Jo looked amazed. Not quite as amazed as when Phil started kicking the ball on the end of his chain, doing keepie-uppie with it.

We should have been cross, but it really made us laugh.

Phil said, "I know, life-like, isn't it? You never know when a rubber ball and chain will come in handy."

Jo punched him on the arm again. Phil said, "You cheeky scamp."

And that's when she got him in a headlock.

Vaisey and Jack quietly sloped off and sat on a tree stump together. Flossie zoned in on Ben, which made his fringe go very floppy. She pinned him against a tree with an arm above his head. This time he looked like a pleased but very startled earwig.

So that just left me and Charlie.

Please don't let me start the mad Irish dancing.

Charlie came closer. "So are you pleased to see us? We made a mad dash for it when the fire alarms went off."

I said, "Yep, I really am glad to see you... It's nice to see you. Did you do anything nice at the weekend?"

Charlie smiled more. "Er, yeah. Not much happened, us being under house arrest. Yourself?"

I said, "Well, yes quite a few things happened. Well two things happened. Well, no it's more like three things happened..."

What am I talking about?

In the distance we heard a dog whistle and Charlie said, "Tallulah, I'm longing to hear about the 'things that happened', I love your 'things', I don't always know what you're talking about, but I love them... but we have to get back now. Hoppy can't keep this punishment thing up for much longer; once he realises that we're all grown-ups and can be trusted we'll be out to play again. Then you can tell me about all the things that have happened."

Jo and Phil were having a serious talk. Then Jo said something and they shook hands.

What was all that about?

Charlie said to the others, "Lads, we need to cut and run. I think Hoppy has realised that the fire in the chimneys is just a smoke bomb."

Vaisey was on cloud nine all day after seeing Jack.

And Flossie said, "Why, ladeez, toying with that boy Ben has perked me up, y'all."

But Jo was a bit funny. Sort of thoughtful, which is unusual in someone so violent.

The next day when I got into Dother Hall, Flossie and Vaisey came scampering out. Jo wasn't with them. Vaisey said breathlessly, "Jo went and gave herself up to Sidone!"

Flossie said, "Yeah, she told us all last night that she was going to do it. She said it wasn't fair that everyone was suffering and that she was going to tell Sidone everything and take her punishment like a man."

I said, "But she's not a man."

Flossie said, "No, but she has an Inner Man, doesn't she? He can take the punishment."

Bob went clanking by. I think he's trying to grow sideburns. He said, "Peace out, dudes."

We didn't see Jo until break. She came to the café looking very downcast. She sat down and said, "Whatever anyone tells you, never, ever tell the truth. It's not worth it. The rest of you are free but my life is over."

Vaisey said, "Sidone hasn't expelled you, has she?!"

Jo said, "No, no, it's far worse than that."

Vaisey put her arm round her. "What is it, Jo? You can tell us, we can help."

Jo said, "No, this is something I simply have to do myself, alone."

Flossie said, "What?"

Jo said, "I've to assist Bob in his duties."

Dear God!! That is harsh.

Jo has to start her new duties immediately. We saw her going off with Bob. He was clanking along, saying, "OK, dude, we'll start with my new insulation idea. I've been collecting eggboxes for some time and I want us to Sellotape them to the windows in the dance studio to keep the heat in. I've seen eggboxes used at Glasto – very cool."

Jo wearily said, "But then it'd be dark all the time, Bob. In fact, it would be pointless having windows, we might as well brick them up."

Bob said, "Hmm, good point, let's keep thinking out of the box – eggbox-wise."

When I got back to Dandelion Cottage, the kitchen was full of wellington boots covered in mud and a bird's nest (probably going to be made into some sort of hat. Or it might already be a hat). Oh and the usual moss and a jam jar with some newts in it.

I shouted out "Helloooo" and Dibdobs shouted from upstairs, "Hellloooo, Lullah, we're all in the bath getting the mud off."

That must be a sight, Dibdobs and the lunatic twins in the bath together!

Then Harold shouted down, "Yes, it's a squeeze, Tallulah, but, it's fun, isn't it, boys?"

There was a lot of splashing and wild laughing from the twins and then Dibdobs shouting, "Now then, Max, get down from the sink because we don't..."

There was an enormous splash and shouting, "Me in my bumbums!!!!!"

Then hysterical laughing from the lunatic twins and shouting from Harold.

"You're being very silly boys! Don't... now look, Sam, this has gone far enough. DO NOT make Dicky dive from the..."

And there was another splash and mad laughing.

I made a sandwich (not out of moss) and took it up to my squirrel room. There was water coming from under the bathroom door. I carefully closed my door to eat my local sandwich in peace.

I can't help thinking about Charlie. It was so nice to see him yesterday. I feel like I can be myself around him. A bit nervy but not entirely mad. I wish I could get to know him better. It's not very likely at this rate. Just bumping into him in the woods now and again. That's more like having an elf for a friend.

Half an hour later it seemed quiet in the bathroom, so I took a chance and went to the loo. Dibdobs was reading a story to the boys in their bedroom. I could hear her saying, "And the big bad wolf said, 'Come nearer, my dear.' And Little Red Riding Hood said, 'Ooooh, Grandma, what a big nose you've got' and the wolf said..."

Sam or Max shouted, "Look at my big bum, it's SJUUUGE!"

Dibdobs shouted, "Boys, will you STOP this silly bum thing."

The boys were hysterical with laughter. Poor Dibdobs.

About eight o'clock I heard the door open and someone come in downstairs. Oh good, it might be Ruby, I could do with some company.

A voice called up, "Harold, are you in? It's Maurice. I've got an unusual leaf mould you might be interested in."

Harold yelled, "I'm on my way down, forager friend!"

Poor, poor Dibdobs. But she doesn't seem to mind Harold and his foraging.

I wonder if they snog, Dibdobs and Harold.

I wonder what number they've got to on my Lulu-Luuuve List?

Oh Angel Gabriel on a tricycle, that's made me feel really embarrassed and hot. I'm blushing, thinking about the 'you know who's' even getting to Number 1 on the Lulu-Luuuve list. I must think about something different.

It seems ages ago that I snogged Charlie. Weeks and weeks, but I can still remember what it felt like.

I know, I'm going to try and recreate the snog on the back of my hand. If I half open my mouth and press it on my hand, I can see what that feels like. Mmm. It's nice. I'll apply a bit more pressure. And move my lips.

Nice. I'm quite good at this. I remember that he slightly put the tip of his tongue on the inside of my lips as he kissed me. I'll try that. Oooooh, it tickles!

Mmmmmmmm. All warm and softy.

I'm going to update my Lulu-Luuuve List with the latest snogging info.

1. *Hand resting*
2. *Corker-holder release*

I wonder for the sake of science if I should include the lunatic twins kissing my knees as Number 3. No that's too weird.

3. Bat kiss or goodnight kiss (with or without a little bat in your mouth)
4. Nose-licking
5. Proper kiss possibly lasting two minutes, with additional praise for knees
   OOOOOHHH, Charlie.
6. Proper kiss with lips, tongues and everything

I woke up in the middle of the night thinking about my Lullah's Lulu-Luuuve List. Should I, for absolute accuracy, add 'mental snogging'? Because that's what I'd done when I kissed the back of my hand and pretended it was Charlie.

Maybe 'mental snogging' should be Number 2 and corker-holder release should be Number 3. Although, if I'm including all of my experiences, should I also include feeling my own corkers with thick winter socks on my hands?

No.

CHAPTER 11
The magic of puppetry

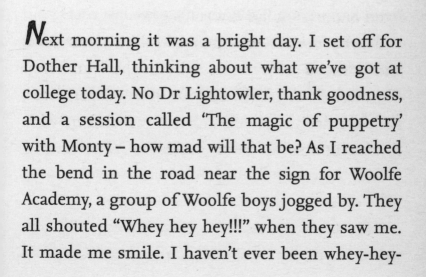

*N*ext morning it was a bright day. I set off for Dother Hall, thinking about what we've got at college today. No Dr Lightowler, thank goodness, and a session called 'The magic of puppetry' with Monty – how mad will that be? As I reached the bend in the road near the sign for Woolfe Academy, a group of Woolfe boys jogged by. They all shouted "Whey hey hey!!!" when they saw me. It made me smile. I haven't ever been whey-hey-

hey-ed by boys before! Then I saw Charlie jogging along. He smiled and waved. "See you soon, Lullah. *Arrivederci!*"

Ahhh. I waved back. That was nice. Really, really nice. I walked on. He really is, well, I'm glad he's on my Lulu-Luuuve List. I'd only gone a bit further when Charlie leapt over a gate and started jogging on the spot next to me. He said, "What a surprise! You'll have to stop following me around, Tallulah."

Then he leaned against the fence. I smiled at him. This was nicer than nice. He said, "So what's been happening, Tallulah, since we last met?"

If only he knew I'd been doing mental snogging with him.

I said quickly, "Oh well, I was thinking about, er, puppets."

He laughed, "Of course you were. Who doesn't?"

I went pink and said, "Only because we're doing 'The magic of puppetry' first lesson."

He stood up again. "Outstanding. Will you promise me that the next time I see you, you'll show me the magic of puppetry? Promise?"

I nodded.

Charlie said, "*Ciao* for now." And he jogged off, but then he stopped and called back, "Hey Lullah!"

And he blew me a kiss.

I felt very perked up when I got to Dother Hall. As we went into the small studio, Jo said, "I don't need a puppet workshop. I'm Bob's puppet. He thinks we might try making coffee tables out of newspaper and flour paste."

Monty was dressed for puppet action in a pink onesie. Like a really big jelly baby. He said, "Now then, girls, things are, well, rather tight at Dother Hall so we'll have to use a little bit of imagination vis-à-vis our puppets."

What he actually meant was that we had to imagine the puppets.

Because there were no puppets.

Vaisey said, "Sir, what do we have instead of puppets?"

Monty said, "Aha, we have OURSELVES. *Regardez vous* the wonder of puppetry."

And he started lifting one arm slowly. Like it was on a string.

Then he floppily let his hand fall until it rested on his hip.

Then he lifted his leg up. And placed it all wobbly over the other one. Like some enormous puppeteer was lifting his leg up with a string.

We began to get the picture.

It doesn't matter what I do, Dr Lightowler thinks I'm deliberately doing it to annoy her.

I was continuing the magic of puppetry by walking along the corridor lifting one leg up and placing it down carefully. Then lifting the other one up and waggling my head around from side to side, like it was on strings.

The others went into the loos. But I was still being a puppet. I put my puppet hand on the outside loo-door handle, but it was too floppy. I tried again with my other floppy puppet hand.

Dr Lightowler said, "What are you doing, Tallulah Casey?"

I said, "Er, well, I was just opening the door as a puppet..."

She said, "You are a silly girl." And she looked at me with her big starey eyes.

Weird.

When the Tree Sisters got out of the loo, I told them about seeing Charlie and him blowing me a kiss. Vaisey squeezed me. "Oooooooh, Lulles, he came to see you specially on purpose. And he blew you a kiss!"

Jo said, "Yada yada yada. Oh yes, Lullah, go on about boys and blowing kisses, why don't you? It's like showing a starving man a chip. No, not a chip. A packet of chips with extra chips on top. And eating them all yourself. That's what it's like for me."

Vaisey said, "Charlie's not a chip." And Jo stomped off. Then Vaisey said, "I'm going to come into the village after college with you, Lulles.

I haven't seen Ruby for ages."

On the way home, I was in such a good, happy mood as Vaisey and I walked along arm in arm. Two Tree Sisters together. Each with our own lululuuuve experiences!

Vaisey wanted to know more about Charlie. "So what about Charlie then? What should you do now? Should you ask him about the girlfriend thing?"

I said, "I don't know. I mean, he's not actually said anything. He hasn't said anything's changed."

Vaisey said, "But he blew you a kiss, didn't he?"

I said, "Well, yes, but you know..."

Just as we got to the end of the path, we heard the village church bells ringing. And when we crossed over the bridge, there was quite a crowd gathering in the churchyard.

What on earth was going on?

As we got nearer, we saw Ruby dancing around with Matilda. She shouted to us, "Ay up, you two, guess what? You'll nivver guess what. Nivver,

nivver in a million, zillion years. Nivver."

I said, "Ruby, why don't you just tell us then?"

She said, "I will. Well, Mrs Bottomley took her gun out this aftie and accidentally shot him."

My heart went cold. I didn't really think she'd do it.

"She's not... she's not... she's not shot..."

Ruby nodded. "She has."

I was numb. "Is he... is he very bad?"

Ruby said, "Oh yes, he'll nivver do the tango again. She killed him."

I said, "Oh no. But, but Cain! I never, never..."

Ruby said, "Ast tha gone a bit soft in the head? I mean the goat. Mr Hinchcliff's goat will nivver do the tango again. Well, it won't do owt again becoz it's deaded. Mrs Bottomley shot it by mistake. There's a big meeting abaht it."

I almost laughed with relief.

Everyone was gathered round the gate to the churchyard. All of the Bottomleys were there, even Beverley who was being held up by her sisters.

I said to Ruby, "She doesn't look like she's lost much weight on her starvation diet."

Ruby said, "Ah know. Her head looks smaller though, dun't it? P'raps she's lost weight from there."

Sometimes I don't know what to say to Ruby.

Oh and the Hinchcliffs were there. Well, Seth and Ruben and I suppose that must be their dad. I'd never seen him before, but you couldn't mistake the family resemblance. He was as dark and brooding as the rest of them. And he was carrying a shotgun. Oh dear.

I wonder where Cain is.

I huddled closer to Vaisey.

Ted Barraclough was standing on one of the gravestones. He had his viking horns on. He shouted above the noise, "Ladles and jellyspoons, order, please, order!!!"

Someone shouted out from the back, "Mine's a pint, Ted."

Ted said, "Most amusing, Isaac, you're barred. Now then, as Champion Pie-eater of Heckmondwhite, I feel it is my duty to sort out this regrettable incident. The shooting and bad mithering has gone on long enough."

Mr Hinchcliff said gruffly, "She's a bloody madwoman. Like all women, she should be locked up."

Mrs Bottomley yelled out, "Dun't start, it were tha bloody wild savage son that started it. Sniffing around my girl, driving her to suicide and—"

Ted said, "Now then, for starters, I want both of you to hand over your weapons. You can have them back when the meeting's over and we've come to some agreement."

Mrs Bottomley and Mr Hinchcliff both yelled out "Over my dead body!" and "Nivver!"

Ted said, "Well, I'd like to say that I hoped it wouldn't come to me PHYSICALLY dealing with the two of you. I'd like to say that, but I dun't mean it. Nothing would give me greater pleasure than smashing your heads together. Hand me my botty-breaker, please, lads."

Ted rolled up his sleeves and one of The Iron Pies handed him a big club. Ted stepped forward. Mrs Bottomley said, "Dun't be hasty, Ted."

Ted said, "Now then, what's it to be?"

Mrs Bottomley handed over her gun. Ted said to Mr Hinchcliff, "Now you. You can have it back when we've sorted this lot out."

Mr Hinchcliff said, "You'd better." And handed over his gun as well.

Ted went back to his gravestone.

"Now then, will the parties concerned step forward? Beverley, if you will, my little luv, and what about Cain?"

Mrs Bottomley said, "He'll not show his face round here, he's not got the gumption."

Beverley burst into tears. Mrs Bottomley said to Mr Hinchcliff, "Look at the state of her, that's his work, the black demon."

Ted said, "Now, now, let's not call names. Beverley, do you want your mother to stop shooting at Cain?"

Mr Hinchcliff said, "I wouldn't bloody mind if she were shooting at Cain, but the way she aims my whole bloody farm will be slaughtered afore she gets him."

Ted said, "Awreet. Beverley, I repeat, do you want your mother to stop shooting at Cain?"

Beverley was hiccuping and sniffing. "Yes, I do. I nivver wanted her to go after him in the first place. We were all right before that posh lass came here to prance around like a tit."

I tried to shrink down behind Ruby. Ted said, "Let's not be unkind to our neighbours the thespians. Isn't that what the Lord says, Beverley, blessed are the thespians?"

Erm, I hadn't actually read that in the Bible.

Ted said to Seth and Ruben, "Nah then, you lads, will you mek an oath that your Cain will not bother Beverley again?"

Seth said, "Our Cain said if he nivver saw Beverley again it would be too soon."

Beverley burst into tears and ran off towards the bridge. Ted shouted after her, "Beverley, I warn thee, I've got me dinner waiting for me. I'm not going in that river again even if you are."

The sisters rushed off after her. Ted went on. "Well, all that remains now is for the respective families to shake hands and for us all to be friends, ordinary normal folk and thespians alike."

The Bottomleys and Hinchcliffs started to leave.

Well, so that's that.

Vaisey said to Ruby as we walked out of the churchyard, "Do you think that'll be it now? You know, like us all living in peace, peace and goodwill to others. Forgive and forget. Love thy neighbours. Treat others as you would wish to be treated?"

Ruby said, "Don't be thick, Vaisey."

We went back to The Blind Pig for tea and Ruby told us that Matilda is going to be The Iron Pies' backing dancer. She said, "I'll show you her in her costume. Don't look until I've put it on her, then you'll get the full effect."

Matilda had gone under the bed – she didn't seem to want her costume on. So for five minutes I was mostly talking to Ruby's bottom as she struggled to get the costume on her.

She was saying, "Matilda! It's nice, you'll like it, you'll love it."

When she eventually dragged Matilda out, Ruby said, "Ta-dah!"

Vaisey and I looked at Matilda in her backing dancer outfit.

I said, "I don't know for sure, but I think this might contravene some European animal rights act."

Surely it's wrong to dress a dog in a ra-ra skirt. Even if it is very, very funny. And has a matching leather cap.

CHAPTER 12
Return of the beast in trousers

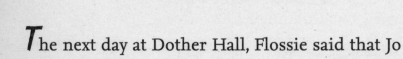

*T*he next day at Dother Hall, Flossie said that Jo has got a special kicking tree in the back garden that she goes to.

No sign of the Woolfe boys; it looks like they're all still under strict surveillance.

This afternoon we have a 'Clown workshop' with Blaise Fox. At last my time to shine. Time to show what I am made of to someone who appreciates me!

The notices we had in our pigeonholes from Blaise gave us an outline of the clowning workshop.

Everyone has an 'Inner Clown' struggling to get out. In this workshop you will discover your own Inner Clown. Bring big hankies as there will be a lot of crying.

Flossie said, "I thought clowns were supposed to make you laugh."

I said, "They don't make me laugh, but then I don't like being chased by someone in big shoes with a feather duster."

Vaisey said, "I don't know what an 'Inner Clown' is. I don't know that I'm a clowny sort of person. Do clowns have curly hair and turny-up noses? Is that what Blaise means?"

She was genuinely thinking about her Inner Clown.

Jo put her arm round Vaisey. "You're a bit mixed up – it's this cold weather and the snow in the lavatory. Your curly hair and turny-up nose is your OUTER Clown. What you must find is the clown that lurks about inside you."

There was a honking noise and Blaise came into the class in a moustache and black lederhosen. She was pointing a stuffed fish at us and yelled, "Don't argue with *zer Fischen*!!!"

So Blaise's Inner Clown is a mad German fishmonger.

Blaise had brought in an enormous box full of props and wigs, false noses, moustaches and fake fur. Also there was another big box that had tambourines and those horns that you press and they go parp parp, and big rubber hammers and ladders, buckets, paintbrushes, traffic cones and all sorts. We started rifling through the boxes.

Jo shoved two horns down the front of her shirt and played *Jingle Bells* on them. She said, "I'm going to keep these and wear them the next time I see Phil. I think he'll like them and they'll make a lasting impression."

She's not wrong.

Flossie went for massive eyebrows and a comedy moustache. She was walking around with bow legs saying, "Howdy doodie."

Blaise stopped in front of Flossie and said, "Well, well, and who is this Inner Clown?"

Flossie shouted, "The name's Hank, ma'am, and I'm lookin' for mah hoss, Andrew. And then we're headin' for the goddam hills, ma'am!!!"

We had to get into twos and "interact in a clowny way" as Blaise said. Vaisey clung on to my arm. Her sweet little face looked all worried.

"I don't really know how to do this, Lulles."

I said, "Stick with me, little pally. If anyone knows how to be a clown, it's me!"

Vaisey and me rummaged in the boxes and found baldy wigs, enormous check trousers and red noses and some hilariously big shoes. And I found some buckets and paintbrushes.

Aha. The very thing.

I said to Vaisey, "You know what we're going to be with these big shoes and buckets, don't you, Vaisey?"

She shook her curls and I popped my red nose on.

I said, "Go get that ladder, Vaisey, we're going to decorate! And whatever I do keep decorating!!"

We set up in business as Coco and Loco, clown decorators. Vaisey got up the ladder and started pretending to paint and I 'helped' by falling over a plank and getting my head stuck in the ladder. When I got my head out of the ladder I fell backwards over my shoes and ended up with my bottom in a bucket.

It was decorating chaos.

In the end everyone was watching us. You name it I fell over it or through it. And what made it even funnier was that Vaisey just went on decorating.

Everyone was laughing at us, but in a good way. As the bell for the end of class rang, Vaisey bowed and I smacked her on the bum with my plank, she put the bucket over my head and I fell into the trunk of props.

Blaise said, "Marvellous, girls. All of you. But top marks, Tallulah! Lullah, you were born to be a clown. I've always said that you had an unusual talent!!!"

Yes!! One nil to me, Dr Lightowler!!

As we went out for break, I said, "Ms Fox, can I ask you something? It's just I winked at Dr Lightowler accidentally and now she thinks everything I do is to annoy her..."

Blaise said, "You winked at Dr Lightowler. I see, I see the trouble. She doesn't understand you. She doesn't understand that you are truly and genuinely daft. It's your special gift. The world must see it."

And she went off.

That's good, isn't it?

I think.

I was exhausted but clown happy on my way home. I was going to go and visit Ruby and Matilda, but I just wanted to have a bath and lie down. As I passed the church, I saw a poster on the door.

Oh, good another 'Foraging Extravaganza –

bring your own bucket' poster by the Dobbins…

But when I went to look closer, the poster had a photograph of the backs of four boys all dressed in black. One doing a rude hand sign. Above them was printed in capitals: **DON'T COME, YOU LOSERS**.

And then at the bottom it said: **The Jones on the twenty-fourth.**

So they were back. Bold as brass. They have no shame, those boys. It didn't take Cain long to get over his near-death experience. He'd be the one in the middle doing the rude sign.

Huh.

I wonder why Vaisey hasn't said anything. She usually tells me everything that Jack's doing. Not that I care. It hasn't anything to do with me, because no way in a hundred years am I going to their stupid gig.

The clown experience has completely worn me out. And I think I might have bruised my bottom, but I'm too tired to look.

I overslept the next morning and had to get a skedaddle on because otherwise I was going to be late. As I was rushing through the front door just in time for assembly, Dr Lightowler beaked along. She looked at me and tutted. Then she did it again!

She winked at me. Just with one eye.

I didn't wink back.

I so wanted to.

Today we're having Sidone's 'Mistress class on *The Taming of the Shrew*'. Monty was already at the lectern when we went in. He has his dance tights on. Flossie said, "Let's sit at the back in case there's any ballet dancing from Monty."

Monty was very excited and as we took our seats he was practically doing the conga. Clapping his hands together for our attention, he said, "Girls, today we have the amazing, the astonishing, the divine Ms Sidone Beaver with her 'mistress class'." And he tinkled with laughter. "Did you see what I did there, girls, did you? It's usually a 'master class', but I said mistress class because Ms Beaver is, well, she's a woman!!!"

I said, "Should we act surprised? I mean, I'd guessed she was a woman all along, didn't..."

And, on cue, Sidone entered stage right in a pussycat mask.

She walked in a pussycat way to the desk and growled at Monty who practically split his tights with delight. He was saying, "Oh, oh, madam, desist, desist!!!"

Sidone took off her mask and fanned herself with it. She addressed us. "What we are striving to reveal to a modern-day audience, girls, is that the battle of the sexes is as savage as it was in the Bard's day."

There was a swift intake of breath from Monty as he tried to sit down on his chair.

Sidone went on. "Kate is depicted as a shrew because she thinks that men seek to disempower her. As indeed she might. You have only to think of me, girls, last term, a delicate woman pitting herself against the bullying male forces of darkness, Mr Smitheebottom the assistant tax inspector."

Monty started sighing, "Aaaaaah, me, Madam, the plague that is my sex."

Sidone wafted herself with her pussycat mask and smiled coyly from behind it, glancing at Monty.

Monty tried to cross his legs carelessly, but sadly his legs were willing, but his tights were not, so he changed it to a sort of scissor-legs effect.

Sidone said to him, "Nay, nay, Mr de Courcy, you are not as other men!"

We all looked at each other and raised our eyebrows.

Sidone went on pacing up and down. "So, girls, how do we stage a play like this? In a modern way. In our way. Mr de Courcy and I will improvise on the theme of male versus female, to give you some ideas."

Monty started to strut around. Pumping his chest out. Vaisey said quietly, "Why is he being a chicken?"

I said, "Perhaps he's feeling a bit peckish."

Sidone stood on the other side of the room, facing Monty. Just watching him and doing acting laughing. He was still chickening about.

Sidone yelled, "Desist, you larrikin! You man!!!"

Monty did a comedy double-take and mid-strut put his hands on his hips. He shouted back, "Fie, madam, a curse on your bustle!"

Sidone stepped towards him shouting, "My bustle? My bustle!!! You rapscallion in tight trousers!"

Monty stepped nearer. "Aha!!! My tight trousers?! A shiny groat for your hard and straining stays, MADAM!"

We watched in amazement as they got nearer and nearer to each other. Shouting insults all the way.

"Prancing poltroon!!!"

"Wittering wench!"

"Lumpy lout!"

"Prattling primpbottom!"

Until they were nose to nose.

And both yelled together, "Touché!!!" and fell into each other's arms.

Sidone said, "Oh, my Petruchio."

And Monty said, "Ah, my sweet Kate."

Flossie whispered, "They're not going to snog, are they?"

And they started to waltz.

Then it was our turn. Half of us had to be boys and half girls. Sadly I'd got Jo as my partner and she said, "I'm the bloke."

She joined the other 'blokes' and I joined the 'ladies'. Insults began flying backwards and forwards across the room. Everyone was really getting into it.

Jo took an enormous step forward and shouted, "I can see your corkers from here!"

I shouted back, "You're not supposed to take such a big step, you loon."

She shouted, "Oh, shut up going on, you lanky streak of lard."

I shouted, "I'm not going on actually, you criminal."

Jo shouted, "I'll give your nose a big lick in a minute."

Oh. Oh.

In a quiet shout I said, "Don't you dare start that."

Jo yelled, "Or what? Show us your corkers!"

I yelled back, "Shut up, you big, you big black crow!"

Jo had got a glint in her eye now. She was so close I could see it. She said, "You know you love it!"

Right, that did it!

"You beast, you animal in trousers!"

Cain, er, I mean Jo, yelled practically nose to nose with me. "If you don't like the animals, don't come into the woods and get hailstones on your nose!!"

I grabbed her round the head. And I was shouting at her. "I'm not a shrew, I'm a human being!!!"

I literally went a bit mad. Even Jo looked frightened. Thankfully Monty rang a bell for time out.

Sidone and Monty were very excited by our performances. Sidone said, "Truly, truly wonderful, girls. The Bard would've been proud of you. Now then, after all that fighting let's all make friends as lovers do."

Jo and I were very red.

Jo said, "Erm, I don't really know where that came from, Lullah. I think I've got cabin fever. I'm sorry."

I said, "Well, I'm sorry for, you know, squashing your head and everything." And we shook hands.

Sidone said, "Right, my girls, I want you to come up with a four-minute piece to be performed in next Friday's lunchtime performance slot. These pieces will make up a third of your marks for the term. Choose different partners. Dig deep, darlings, and come to the banquet with the fruits of your psyches!"

Fruits of our psyches?

As we walked out to lunch, Vaisey came up to me

and said shyly, "Lullah, you know this performance assessment piece, well, would you do it with me? I'd really like us to do something together, you know, because, well, the clown thing was good, wasn't it?"

Oh this was nice, people wanting to work with me. Vaisey said, "Let's go for a little walk on our own and talk about everything."

We got togged up and went out. Jo had gone off to the potting shed and Flossie was in the music studio, so it was just us.

Vaisey said, "Jo has made a shrine to Phil in the potting shed. She eats her biscuits in there and looks up at the boy-shaped hole in the roof."

I said, "Does she offer him a biscuit?"

Vaisey said, "No, but she sometimes tells him about her day."

As we got into the woods, Vaisey burst out, "Tallulah, something happened that was so, so nice. Well, after supps last night, I went out to get fir cones for my *Taming of the Shrew* collage and guess what, Jack was in the woods!!!"

She was beside herself with excitement.

"He said he came in the hope that he might see me!! He jogged over to the woods and jogged about for ages and he said he felt my presence. And there I was!!"

Ahhhh.

"What happened?"

Vaisey blushed. "Well, he told me about some new tunes he's been practising and then he told me that The Jones are coming to our music studio tomorrow to rehearse for their gig."

I said, "Oh."

Vaisey carried on. "Only nobody must know because of, you know, the trouble there's been. Jack's got special permission from Hoppy to be there. It's a big secret. So we're sworn to secrecy, aren't we? Flossie and Jo have already promised."

I said, "Yeah, of course. Did you just talk to Jack then? Or was it a bit more physical than that? Was there any progress on the Lulu-Luuuve List?"

Vaisey went double red and nodded. I put my arm round her and squeezed her.

She said, "I think we're getting good at kissing now. It's all practice, isn't it? I mean, at first you don't know where to put your hands, do you? And you don't want to knock teeth or anything."

I said, "Hmmm, that's a good point. Where should they go, do you think?"

Vaisey was chewing a curl. "How do you mean, Lulles? Where should your teeth go? I…"

"No, Vaisey, I mean HANDS. Where were Jack's hands when you were snogging?"

"Erm, I think they were, well, on the top of my top bottom."

"On the top of your top bottom – where's that?"

Vaisey turned round and put her hands on her bottom. "Here, not on the bottomy sticky-out bit, just as it begins to stick out."

I must remember the hands position for the future. Maybe I should have a bit on my list about hand positions.

Vaisey said, "What else do you want to know?"

I thought and then said, "Has Jack done, I mean, does he ever, you know, do open mouth and tongue stuff at the same time?"

Vaisey said, "Not so far. Should he, do you think? Did you do that with Charlie?"

I said without thinking, "No, not with Charlie but..."

Uh-oh.

Vaisey looked puzzled. "Then who...?"

And it all came out in a rush. "It was out on the moors last term, and it was, well, he kissed me, properly, with tongues and everything."

Vaisey said, "On the moors? Tongues? Whose tongues?"

I looked down at the ground. She put her arm round me. I had to tell someone.

I said, "The nose-licker's tongue."

Vaisey shouted, "Cain?! Cain??!"

I nodded.

She looked at me and shouted, "Cain!"

I said quietly, "Vaisey, that's not the worst of it... It was so nice, I thought I was melting."

Vaisey said, "Oh noooooo, Lullah – no – the Rusty Black Crow of Heckmondwhite. Did you get that thing about not knowing which way up you were or where his mouth starts and yours ends and..."

I was nodding. "Yes – but I hate Cain. He's hateful. He laughs at me and humiliates me."

Vaisey gave me a hug. "His bark's probably worse than his bite. He says things he doesn't really mean. Jack says he's got an artistic temperament."

"Vaisey, he's not doing a dance or painting when he says horrible things to me, he just says them. I think he hates me."

"How can he not love you, Lullah? You've got lovely hair and your eyes and everything."

"What about my legs?"

Vaisey paused for just a bit too long. "Yes, yes, and your legs."

"Vaisey, do you mind if we don't talk about this any more? It's making me feel sad and strange."

Vaisey said, "Look, no one needs to know anything about the Cain thing."

I said, "Accidental Number 6 on Lullah's Lulu-Luuuve List?"

Vaisey said, "Yes. When The Jones come to college you can act like a normal person, you know, all casual."

I said, "Oh I see what you mean. Sort of cool – I mean, it's just a band, isn't it? Everyone knows what I think about Cain."

Vaisey bounced her curls around, gave me another big hug and said, "Exactly – I won't tell."

As we walked back to Dother Hall, she said, "Hey, I've got a secret Curly Wurly we can share. I wanted to ask you something special about the duet." She handed me a bit of Curly Wurly. Yum yum.

I said, "Fire away."

She was pulling at her curls like mad. I was glad we were changing the subject to something more cheerful. "What did you have in mind, little curly pal?"

Vaisey said, "Well, Jack says that when he drums he puts all of himself into it and he doesn't hold back... he... feels the rhythm in his soul."

I began to get worried.

"We're not, I mean, you don't want me to do a drumming duet, do you? Because you remember the last time when we did ad hoc drumming and my leg went through the stage and there was a..."

Vaisey put her hand on my arm and smiled. "No, not drumming. He says we've all got something inside, like a secret that we feel vulnerable about. But that can be our best bit."

I said, "For a boy, Jack is very wise."

"Oh, I knew you'd understand, Lullah. I think you're the best pal I've ever had. You've always understood me. Do you remember when we first met and I showed you how I used to ride my pretend horsey to school?"

I laughed. "Yeah, that was bonk—"

"And you didn't laugh at me, you sort of understood."

I changed my face to an understanding one.

Vaisey was quite worked up. "And so I want to do something that's about my childhood, something that really means something, something other people might not understand. And I thought of you."

I hugged her. "Yes, you and me, Vaisey. This will be an opportunity to put the Sugar Plum Bikey fiasco firmly behind us."

She said, "I wondered if you'd be Merrylegs in my Black Beauty piece."

Doomed, I am doomed.

As I walked home later, I thought, *everything is coming back to haunt me.*

The Dark Rusty Crow of Heckmondwhite is back, and now so are my long lanky legs.

Held up to the cruel audience of life.

And what is more, this time when I show them in public... there will be four of them!

CHAPTER 13
See you there, cheeky miss

On Monday, I arrived at Dother Hall desperate to go to the loo. Because Dibdobs gave me some of her special foraging tea that's made out of dried dandelions and squirrel poo or something. I haven't been able to stop going to the loo since. And my pee is green. But thankfully not full of acorns.

I can see why Ted Barraclough calls it Dither Hall. I couldn't get into the loos for girls putting on lipstick and hitching their skirts up this morning.

What was going on?

Milly said, "Exciting, isn't it, about The Jones coming?"

How did she know?

I said, "They're not."

Milly said, "Oh yes they are, Flossie said."

It wasn't just in the loos, it was all around the school that The Jones were coming. When I met up with the Tree Sisters in the café, I said to Flossie, "Everyone I asked said you and Jo had told them about The Jones."

Flossie said, "Oh yeah."

Vaisey said to Jo, "But it was a secret. Jack might get into trouble because Hoppy said…"

Jo said to Vaisey, "Hoppy smoppy!!! You don't understand what it's like to not see boys for ages and ages. I haven't seen Phil; I'm like a nun. I've got excess boy energy to work off. I've had to listen to Bob tell me about his new drum solos for a week, in between unbunging drains and… Come on, if you're so upset about Flossie and me telling people, let's fight!! I'll take you all on."

And she pushed Vaisey over and then leapt on my back and started giddying me up like a donkey.

As we all went into assembly, Jo was still on my back, despite this, I started my casually disinterested plan. I said to Flossie, "Honestly, don't you think it's pathetic? It's just, just the Hinchcliffs and Jack when it comes down to it. Just you know, just a bunch of boys, playing songs and moaning about life. They'll probably fall out by about half past two and break Bob's sound equipment."

Vaisey squeezed my hand and gave me a secret look. And Flossie said, "I completely understand, Miss Lullah. But ditch the small mad person on your back and get your lip gloss out! I've run out and that Seth boy is in for a meeting he won't never forget!"

I shoved Jo off and whispered to Vaisey, "I don't – I can't – I don't want to see Cain."

Vaisey squeezed my hand again. "Look, we can hide at the back and creep off…"

After second period, I was walking along to the art studios and passed a mass of girls screeching outside the front door. Flossie came out of the loos again. How much lip gloss can one person apply? She grabbed my hand and dragged me along with her. I said, "Flossie, what are you doing? I don't want to…"

She dragged me to the front of the crowd just as Seth appeared with his guitar over his shoulder. He stopped right in front of her. She stood there looking back at him. Someone, I think it might have been Milly, shouted, "I love you, Seth."

Without looking away from Flossie, Seth said, "You're only human, love."

Milly said, "Thank you."

I tried to get my hand away from Flossie's but she held on tight. She's big and wasn't going to move. The girls hushed. Seth put his head down and swished back his dark hair. He looked up and licked his lips.

"My, looking good, Florence. Where's tha been hiding tha sen?"

Uh-oh.

The girls around them edged away slightly. Flossie took off her glasses and thrust her face towards him as if she was going to kiss him. Blimey.

Then she said, "I've been hiding from you, you big rough thing."

And she clicked her fingers and turned away.

Haha! That'll teach him.

I followed her through the crowd of girls as the bell rang for musical drama.

I said, "Yeah, yeah, good work, see how a Hinchcliff likes that."

Flossie didn't say anything. I went on. "Yeah, you showed him, the way you said you'd been hiding from him. That'll be the last time Seth bothers you."

Flossie said slowly, "Oh no, no... you'll see, he

loves that sort of thing."

What sort of thing?

Jo said, "Where is the Dark Black Crow of Heckmondwhite? Has Mrs Bottomley shot him?"

Vaisey said, "Oh no, Jack says he's always late. He'll be here. Did you see me pretending I hadn't seen Jack? He was pretending that he hadn't seen me and I was pretending I hadn't seen him and..."

Monty came bustling by and interrupted us. "Girls, girls, what larks we'll have today in our musical drama lesson!!"

I didn't know that Monty knew the whole of *We Will Rock You* but he does.

It's quite soothing in a way when he gives a lecture because we can all have a rest while he does tap dance, air guitar, songs, 'modern dance' etc. and we just marvel at how his trousers don't split.

Still, at least it distracted me from my own head for an hour.

I know that Cain is somewhere in the building. I can sort of 'feel' his presence. And it's not a nice feeling, it's a slightly sicky feeling. But anyway, as Vaisey says, I don't need to see him. The Jones will probably have fallen out by now and gone off for a fight in the woods.

At mid-afternoon break, I passed the music studios to see girls crowded around reading a notice. Handwritten by Bob in red, it said:

Ears on!!
No backstage access.
Musos at work.
Bob
(technician, musician, Dudemeister)

At the end of the day, practically the whole of my year was waiting by the studio door. I was trying to push my way through to the dormitory stairs. If I went and lurked up there, The Jones would leave and then I could safely go home. Milly was hopping about with Tilly. "Lullah, they're coming out, they're coming out!"

Lav, Dav and Noos ambled along. Lav saw me and came over specially to ruffle my hair. "Top of the day to you, Oirish. Have you come to see the young men?"

I said, "No, not at all, I was just... getting my coat."

Lav ruffled my hair again. Why does she do that? It's like she's patting a big dog.

She said, "Ah, you're 'getting your coat', are you? To be sure, to be sure. Are you keeping it in the music studios, me dahling?"

And she went off tinkling with laughter with Dav and Noos.

Bob came clanking through the swing doors from the studio shouting, "OK, cool it, dudettes. Let them through. No autographs. The band have to make their way to a gig. So move along."

Everyone just kept on jumping up and down and screeching. Bob adjusted his trousers which were coming adrift with the weight of his spanners and shouted again, "OK, listen up.

You dudes know my band The Iron Pies, well, breaking news, our next gig is at the Cattle Market in Cleckheaton! I have some flyers here which I can sign for you, if you form an orderly queue."

Jack appeared through the doors followed by Ruben and Cain, and Bob was practically flattened in the stampede. As soon as I saw Cain, that old dread feeling came over me. He was dressed all in black and immediately surrounded by girls, asking him to sign their pencil cases and their arms. Cassie Perkins actually fainted and had to be taken to the sickbay by Gudrun.

I glanced back at Cain who was looking down, signing something, and as I did, Cain looked up, over the heads of all the adoring girls.

Straight at me.

How had he known to look up just then?

A second later and I would have been gone.

He's like a wild animal. He seems to sense where I am.

Then, as the girls started pulling at his jacket,

Ruben and Jack dragged him off through the crowd.

Flossie was just by me and she said, "He looked straight at you, didn't he? That baaaaaaad Cain boy."

Then Seth came through the swing doors from the studio with his guitar. Flossie said, "Well, well, well, speaking of bad boys."

She stood still and looked at Seth. He noticed her. Then he handed his guitar to Bob and pushed his way through the girls until he was standing in front of Flossie.

I tried to back away. All of the girls went quiet.

Seth said, "I've got summat for thee, big lass."

Flossie put her hands on her hips.

"Oh, what could you possibly have that I'd want?"

And he winked at her and handed her a poster. He said, "It's got my picture on it."

Flossie said, "Is it a 'Wanted' poster issued by the police?"

Seth put his face closer to hers. "It's the poster for our gig. Why don't tha come? I'd like to see more of thee. There's a lot of thee to see, isn't there?"

Flossie smiled and then ripped up the poster in front of him.

Ruben shouted from the crush at the door, "Seth, get your daft arse out here."

Seth said to Flossie, "Yabba dabba do, big girl."

And pushed his way out.

What did that mean?

What did anything mean?

Jo had disappeared off, but she came back and said, "I managed to sneak a note to Jack for Phil. I've outlined my special plan in it so that we can meet again."

I said, "What is the special plan?"

Jo tapped her nose. "Him and me are going to act normal and nice. Pretend we're just like anyone else, and that the potting-shed thing was, you know, an accident that was waiting to happen."

As she went off, I thought yes, well, good luck with that plan.

I hurried home that night feeling a bit shaken up. All this time and now he was back, the Rusty Dark Crow of Heckmondwhite.

Why did he have to come back and do that looking thing?

What did he want?

Maybe he didn't want anything. He just happened to look up.

Anyway, he's probably kissed a hundred girls since, well, since the thing happened.

I've got nothing to worry about. He'll think I'm just another notch on his... microphone stand.

So, good. That's that then.

I can throw the poem away and get on with life.

Get on with thinking about real boys.

Boys who are nice to me. Boys like Charlie.

I wonder if the Woolfe boys will be set free soon.

In the early evening after tea (nettle soup), I thought I'd just have a look around the back woods and see if there's any sign of little Lullah and little Ruby. As I went down the lane, I passed the tree at the bottom of the Dobbins' garden. Where Cain stuck his stupid poem. Which I will be throwing away when I get in.

There was a poster on the tree.

It was The Jones poster.

What a stupid place to put a poster.

Well, not stupid if you wanted to attract voles and squirrels to your gig but... I'm going to take it down.

As I ripped it off, I noticed something handwritten at the bottom. It hadn't been on the other posters. It was written in felt tip.

And I knew the handwriting.

Handwriting that looked like it had been done by someone with a hoof.

Cain's writing.

It said, **See you there, cheeky miss**.

What? Why? What does he want with me?

I took the poster back to Dandelion Cottage and slipped it on to the fire because there was no one in the kitchen.

I was all restless and wound up, so I was glad when Ruby came round with Matilda and we went out again. Even though it was dark it wasn't very cold. She said, "I thought I saw little Lullah and Ruby on my way home from school, so let's go up the back and see."

Matilda went toddling off in front, sniffing at every bit of poo she came across. Ruby said, "Duck poo's her favourite."

I told Ruby about The Jones coming to Dother Hall and what Seth had said to Flossie, but I didn't tell her about the poster. She said, "If I were Seth, I'd be a bit frightened of Flossie."

I said, "I think he likes her being 'off' with him. He said that he was sick of all the 'milky local girls' and that Flossie was a 'cracking snogger' and had a 'strong right hand'."

Ruby said, "Is Flossie a cracking snogger then? I am."

I'm not going to encourage Ruby by saying anything.

But she went on anyway. "You should know if she's a cracking snogger because you told me that the Tree Sisters did practise snogging together."

Did I?

But then fortunately Matilda stopped and started barking at something in the ditch. Well, not barking because she can't really bark – it's more loud snuffling.

Ruby was excited. "She must have found them. Oh, GOOD girl, good girl, you've found them."

And we both ran down the lane. But when we got there, it was a carrot that Matilda was barking at.

Ruby said, "She dun't even like carrots."

Matilda started eating it.

It's sad that the owlets have gone. I said to Ruby, "I wrote a rap song about the owlets leaving, do you want to hear it?"

She said, "No. Me dad's written a rap song for The Iron Pies. It goes:

I'll not lie
I like a pie
But I like my toast and
I'm off just now for me Sunday roast."

What a week and it's still only Wednesday. Dr Lightowler has been appearing unexpectedly, just looking at me wherever I've been. The other terrible thing has been that Jo has started her 'plan'. She is being 'good'.

You wouldn't think any fool would fall for it, but she called Monty "Mr de Courcy" yesterday and asked him to tell her all about his theatre career. Serves her right that he took her seriously and she had to go and have a lie-down after two hours. With a piece of ice (chipped out of the sink) on her head.

She's trying 'being good' with everyone.

Helping carry Gudrun's books.

Doing voluntary dance lessons with the

younger girls in her own time.

Tidying the library.

Volunteering for things.

Being enthusiastic.

Even Dr Lightowler said she thought her interpretation of Kate fighting with Bianca (me) "was quite remarkably vigorous". Too true. I'm covered in bruises.

And also, Dr Lightowler seems to get madder by the moment. She only has to look at me to start blinking and twitching. It's hardly my fault that during the Kate and Bianca fight Jo pushed me on to Dr Lightowler's lap.

Today – Thursday – at break, Jo called us all to a meeting on the roof. Which was freezing.

She said, "I've written an official letter of apology to Sidone. As Bob says, 'put your ears on'."

I said, "I won't have any ears to put on if we stay out here in minus a hundred degrees for much longer."

Jo said, "Shhhh..." and started reading out her letter.

"*Dear Ms Beaver,*

I hope in the last couple of weeks, I have been able to show you and the wonderful teachers here at Dother Hall (Flossie nearly swallowed her Jammie Dodger whole) *my deep regret for the 'potting-shed' incident.*

I of course deserve my punishment and have been only too pleased to help Bob with his maintenance jobs. The new manure heap will, I know, have a lasting effect on future generations of students. And nearby homes.

And of course I accept the embargo on contact outside the college, though I have missed the supportive community of Heckmondwhite.

However, I do feel I should say that in the case of the boy concerned – I believe his name is 'Phillip' – I need to disclose something that I know he never would. And no matter what my fate, I know I am doing the right thing. Because this is a crime of my own making.

It was after we had had your inspiring talk about The Taming of the Shrew. *Of course I was fired up* with ideas, I'm young, I love the theatre, what can I say? Anyway, when I accidentally met with some of the Woolfe boys shortly afterwards, I said that modern boys were not as noble as Petruchio who would have taken any risk to prove himself a man. That someone like Petruchio would, for instance, have climbed any barricade to get to a woman he was interested in.

I thought little more of the conversation. But, to my endless regret, 'Phillip' (I think that may be his name) took me at my word. He wanted to show his mettle. He meant to appear at the dorm window and leave a sausage as a sign that he had been there and then secretly steal away. Having disturbed no one and proved his point. But, as we know, his visit was no secret.

I hope you will find it in yourself to explain to the headmaster of Woolfe Academy that I am responsible. And that I hope 'Phillip' and the other innocent boys will not be punished any further for my crazy obsession with theatre. I do indeed know the proper meaning of bleeding feet.

Yours with deep shame,
Joanna"

We all said that never, ever in a million years would anyone be stupid enough to fall for this.

As she went off to Ms Beaver's office with her letter, Jo said, "Have you met Sidone?"

I cannot believe this. No one can believe it.

Sidone made an announcement in assembly. She said, "Girls, I received a profoundly affecting letter yesterday. I don't need to name names, but suffice it to say this letter reminded me of my own youthful passion for life! For art! For adventure! It seems that the 'potting-shed incident' as I believe it will be known in Dother Hall history" – she chuckled – "was merely the result of youthful *joie de vivre*. So, as of now, all girls are free to come and go as normal."

Everyone cheered!!!

And Jo did a special dance with Bob.

I told Vaisey in private about Cain's note on the

poster and that I wasn't going to go to the gig. She said, "Lullah, we'll be there with you. Don't let stupid Cain stop you seeing your mates and being normal."

And that is why we're all going to The Jones's gig on Saturday night!

CHAPTER 14
My inner snogger

On Saturday evening, my squirrel room looked like backstage at the Oscars. Make-up everywhere and growing hysteria. Even the lunatic twins were covered in lipstick by the time we'd got ready. Then they brought their tortoises up to have some lipstick put on.

I don't know if you've ever tried to get a tortoise to put its head out of its shell so you can apply lip gloss, but they don't like it.

At seven-thirty, we set off across the green to the church hall. Jack had smuggled a note to Vaisey to say that the Woolfe boys are allowed to come to the gig. But they have a quarter-past-eleven curfew when the sports master will meet them to walk them back.

We are all giddy gerties with excitement.

I said to the Tree Sisters, "I know it's silly, but I'm really looking forward to seeing Charlie. I hope he'll be there. I know he's got a tiny girlfriend so I'm only looking forward to seeing him just as a mate."

Jo said, "Yes, I can see that – the sort of mate who's bought a new lip gloss and done double mascara application with sparkly eyelashes. That sort of mate."

Vaisey put her arm through mine.

"Shhh, Jo. I think you look lovely Lullah, with your sparkly eyes and your shiny black hair."

Flossie said, "I don't think it's Charlie that you should be thinking about. I think the nose-licker likes you. I saw him looking at you after rehearsal."

I didn't know what to say so I looked at Vaisey.

Vaisey went bright red and Flossie saw it. She said, "Oy – what's going on? Why is your head about to drop off, Vaisey?"

Vaisey said, "I don't know."

Jo got interested then. "You don't know why your own head is going to drop off?"

Vaisey looked at me for help.

Flossie saw that as well and said, "Why are you looking at Lullah?"

And Jo said, "And why is Lullah's head now going to drop off?"

I couldn't take it any more.

Vaisey looked like she was going to faint.

So I told them all in a rush about the tongue incident on the moors.

Flossie said, "You've secretly done Number 6 with the Dark Black Crow of Heckmondwhite?" Then Jo leapt on me and shouted, "You are an animal in tights!"

So that's it. The Tree Sisters know my worst secret. They know about my Inner Clown and now they know about my Inner Snogger.

As we walked over to the church hall I said, "Well, I'm glad I've told you. Now I can just get it all out of my head and get on with my life."

Flossie said, "Do you think we could stop talking about your head for one minute and talk my boy plan."

Vaisey said, "What boy plan?"

Flossie pushed Vaisey quite hard and said, "Oooooh, you little japester – you know what plan. Me-using-Ben-as-my-decoy-to-get-Seth's-attention plan."

Flossie's 'plan' is to make Seth think that she likes Ben so that he'll be jealous.

I said, "Is that really fair to Batboy?"

Flossie said, "I sure don't want to bring this up, Miss Lullabelle, but you were the one who first trapped Batboy in the sweet nectar of your lips."

Uurrgh!

Wow, the church hall looked like a proper gig.

It had flashing lights and a bar and a 'chill-out space' full of beanbags. Which were supposed to be for lying on when you'd been dancing, but already the rough village lads were hitting each other with them.

Typical.

It was heaving. In fact, it looked like most of the village was there. But when we arrived, it went quiet like in a Western film. You know, when the sheriff walks in through the swing doors and all the cowboys stub out their fags and start feeling for their guns.

I'm not saying the village people had guns. But they all stopped talking and looked at us. Then a stray dog came and sat down beside us. So it was the whole village versus the Tree Sisters and a Labrador.

Where were all the other Dother Hall girls?

And the Woolfe boys?

Flossie said, "Oh Lordy, Lordy."

Vaisey whispered, "Don't look at them, pretend we're talking."

I said, "We are talking."

Jo said, "No, I know what Vaisey means. Nod your heads a lot. I'll start." And she said loudly and slowly, "Erm, it'll be brillage when Phil and the boys get here, won't it?"

We all said, "Yeah, yeah, yeah."

Nod, nod, nod.

Jo said, "Do you think I should snog Phil or wait for him to snog me?"

We nodded.

She said, "What does that mean?"

We nodded again.

She said, "Look, one nod for me and a double nod for him."

But then we all got mixed up so it was more or less continual nodding. The rest of the villagers started talking again and the dog wandered off.

After a few more minutes of nodding, I said, "I really do hope someone comes soon because my neck's about to snap off."

Then we heard chanting outside. "We want fun and we want it now!!!!"

Practically the whole of Woolfe Academy crashed through the doors. Quickly followed by a gaggle of Dother Hall girls. Phil was leading the chanting.

When he saw Jo, he rushed over to her and snogged her! People yelled "Whey hey!!!"

Then Phil shouted to Jo, "Behave yourself, madam! Please be gentle with me."

Jo hit him with her bag, leapt into his arms and the party began.

I knew most of the boys from Woolfe by sight and said hello to Edward and Robin and Ben and John and James and Elton and a few others. But there was no Charlie.

I wonder why?

I noticed Flossie fluttering her eyelashes at Ben and you could see his fringe getting excited. Vaisey said, "Lullah, can you see Jack anywhere? And where's Charlie?"

I didn't know.

Vaisey said she was going to the loo, but I know she was actually seeing if Jack was around anywhere.

Then I saw Ruby! What was she doing here? She must have sneaked in. If her dad finds out, he'll get the botty-breaker out.

Ruby was on one of the beanbags talking to a boy; she had loads of make-up on and you could see her knickers. I must go and get her.

Before I could, Bob clanked by. He was wearing a bandana and had so many torches and appliances attached to his belt I was amazed he could walk. I said to Flossie, "What's Bob doing here?"

Flossie said, "Maybe he's getting down with the kids."

As he passed, I said, "Hello, Bob, what are you doing here?"

Bob said, "I'm helpin' me brethren."

What is he talking about?

Vaisey came back from the loos and said, "Bob's a roadie for The Jones."

Then Bob spotted Ruby and I heard him say, "That is, like, totally not cool. 'Scuse me, brother, I'm on a mission." And he clanked over to Ruby, picked her out of the beanbag and put her under his arm.

As he was carrying her to the door, I could hear her shouting in a French accent, *"Oh là là, m'sieur,* why are *vous* holding *moi* under *votre* fat arm? I am from *la belle France..."*

Bob said, "Ruby, be cool, dudette. It's like not happening for you to be here. The big man, the Piemaster, has rules, and his rule is that you do not bust the gig. You are officially leaving the building."

As she went past, I said, "Night-night, Ruby."

Someone laughed behind me. "Ah, Tallulah, I see our little friend is being carried out early on."

And it was Charlie! Hurrah hurrah. I felt all goofy and wobbly.

Charlie seemed happy to see me. And he looked lovely. In a really sharp suit with a Fred Perry shirt underneath. I like that he's quite tall. And handsome. And lovely. I knew I should say something. But...

He smiled at me. "Can I get you anything from the bar?"

I said, "Yes, that would be, er, as long as it's not a... a... an ice-cube bucket."

Charlie said, "I'll make it a Coke, shall I?" And he laughed and went off.

Wow. This was good. After a shaky start, maybe it was going to be a good evening. Even if Charlie did have a girlfriend, I could still enjoy seeing him.

Then Jack arrived. Hurray! Vaisey lit up like a firecracker. All smiley and dimply.

Jack gave Vaisey a little kiss on her ear and said, "Hello, Vaisey. You look lovely. I'm off to get ready to play. But I'll see you after, won't I? You'll watch me, won't you? I've got new sticks."

Vaisey shook her curls and he went off. She said to me, "He's got new sticks."

I said, "So far he's the only one of The Jones to arrive. They're supposed to be on in ten minutes. Not that I care."

Flossie said, "Oh, is that right, Miss Lullabelle? You just kiss 'em and leave 'em."

Oh no, was the whole night going to be like this?

Just at that moment I caught the eye of one of the village girls. She gave me the evils and said something to her mate who laughed. I hope they don't want a fight.

How do girls fight?

Jo will know.

I caught sight of Charlie surrounded by Dother Hall girls. I could see him laughing and joking. He seems really confident around girls.

Hmmm, that will be because he's had a tiny girlfriend for most of his life.

Vaisey said, "He's popular, Charlie, isn't he? And sporty and good-looking. Gosh, girls really like him, don't they? Look at that Natasha, she's really flirting with him. And those two sisters that live next to the village shop, they're all over him like a rash."

I said, "Yes, yes, Vaisey, I can see that!"

Was he flirting back?

I didn't have time to see what was going on because then the Hinchcliffs arrived. Cain, as usual, the last and at the back. All in black leather. He's incredibly good-looking in an awful way. They're handsome boys, but so moody and difficult. And cross all the time.

There was silence as they arrived and then the village crowd started chanting, "The Jones, The Jones, The Jones."

Seth and Ruben half smiled and raised an acknowledging hand. As they came close to us, Seth made a clicking sound at Flossie. She went cross-eyed.

Cain walked right past and didn't even look at me, just said, "There you are. Tha can't stay away, can thee?"

Flossie said, "Phwoar. He's wearing Eau de Phwoar!"

The Jones pushed through the mob and the barman handed them drinks.

Cain leaned against the stage and looked around. Staring at people from under his lashes. Not talking to his brothers. A few of the lads clapped him on the shoulder or shook his hand as they went by.

A couple of the village girls were giggling and flicking their hair in front of him. As I watched, one said something to him. And he looked at her and lowered his lashes. Then he leaned over and said something in her ear. And it looked like he put his hand on her corker briefly.

He couldn't have done!

Then Cain said something in the other girl's ear and she went all smiley and stupid. What is the matter with some girls?

Ruben tapped Cain on the shoulder and they went off backstage. Jo and Phil still had their arms wrapped round each other and Phil shouted, "I'm free. I'm free! Thanks to my girlfriend!"

Jo looked quite pleased. In fact, I know she was pleased because she hit him hard on the arm.

The background music was cut and Bob came onstage, went to the microphone and tapped it. "Testing, testing. Are you receiving me, dudes?"

Everyone started booing and yelling, "Get off!"

As the booing went on, the Bottomley sisters came in. All four of them in leather coats,

Beverley in the middle. She looked around and caught my eye.

It's official. She hates me.

Flossie said, "Ouch."

Bob shouted through the microphone, "Gentlemen and ladies, and of course all you other dudes. Tonight is going to be mega."

The big lads in the crowd shouted, "Get 'em off!"

And Bob said, "Yeah, nice one. Coolio. But we all know why we're here tonight."

The same big lad said, "Aye, we know why we're here, it's just you we're puzzled abaht."

Bob said, "Brilliant. We've come to see one of the best bands in Yorkshire. They're going to rock our world, they are The Jones!"

Seth, Ruben and Jack came onstage and everybody went mad.

Jack lifted up his sticks and Vaisey shouted, "He said he'd do that, he said he'd show me his sticks, that's what he's doing now."

Ruben tuned up and Seth adjusted his

guitar strap. Then the Dark Black Crow of Heckmondwhite walked on. The crowd were yelling and jumping up and down. Cain walked slowly up to the mike then looked out at the crowd pogoing in front of him.

He said into the mike. "Who are we, who are we???"

And the crowd roared back, "The Jones! The Jones!"

Cain said, "Reight, that's who we are. This is a quiet romantic number called *Get someone else and leave me alone.*"

And the band kicked off at full volume.

Phil shouted above the thrashing guitars and mad drumming. "You can say what you like about Cain, but he can shout loud."

It's true.

He put absolutely everything into it. He was twirling his mike on its lead high up into the air and catching it. He kicked against the drums. He growled and snarled his way through the first song.

I couldn't see Charlie anywhere. Perhaps he'd forgotten about getting me a drink.

Flossie yelled, "I don't think Cain rates girls much, do you?"

As she said that, he announced moodily, "This one is for women everywhere, it's called *Girls like you should be shot.*"

Flossie raised her eyebrows at me. So the only thing to do was DANCE!

Charlie came back and handed me a Coke and tried to say something, but I couldn't hear what it was. So we just shrugged, smiled at each other and danced. Other people joined in, so I got separated from Charlie.

Girls really do like him. He's a cool dancer.

When The Jones kicked into *You are poison,* some of the village lads made a circle and took it in turns to go into the centre on their own to show off their moves. One quite big lad actually did the splits. His mates had to help him up.

After three or four village lads had done their turn, Phil walked into the centre of the circle. The village lads looked like they were going to attack him, but Phil coolly rolled up his sleeves. He walked right round with his arm up.

Jo said, "What's he doing? Has he got a death wish?"

Then Phil dropped down on to his haunches and started doing Cossack dancing.

Jo was clapping Phil on, shouting, "Woolfe, Woolfe!!!!"

What a hoot! I was having so much fun I had forgotten about the band. But then they stopped playing and left the stage. Cain nodded to the two girls he'd been talking to and they giggled and made their way backstage. The black-hearted swine. I know what he's up to.

Not that I care.

I could see Beverley had noticed what he was up to as well. And she was telling her sisters. There's bound to be a fight sooner or later. Good. At least it won't involve me.

I was so hot I staggered to a beanbag and flopped into it. I may never get out of it again.

Ooooh, it was so nice to be in such a comfy big...

Charlie came and flopped down next to me. He said, "Cor."

And I said, "I know."

He smiled at me and lay back. He said, "This is the life. It's like, well, it's like..."

I said, "Sitting in a bag of beans?"

And he smiled back and said, "Exactly."

He was about to say something else when Flossie came and crashed down next to us. I said, "Where's Vaisey?"

And Flossie said, "Looking at Jack's sticks, if you know what I mean."

Ben came along, flopping his fringe, and stopped by Flossie. "Erm, would you like, would you like..."

And Flossie said, "Oh yes indeedy, I would like." And she patted her beanbag.

Ben lowered himself down next to her. He seemed mesmerised by Flossie.

She looked over his shoulder and winked at me. Charlie saw the wink and he raised his eyebrows.

Then Seth came by and, as he did, Flossie pulled Ben towards her and kissed him.

Oh my God.

She was doing it. She was using Ben like a decoy duck. I mean decoy bat. She was doing her decoy bat plan. I wonder if he was doing the bat tongue thing now.

Charlie said to me, "Ben's fringe is bound to drop off."

Seth had stopped and was looking down.

Flossie stopped kissing Ben and looked up at Seth.

Ben didn't look anywhere. He seemed to have gone into a coma. He had his eyes shut and he was in the same position as he'd been when Flossie was kissing him.

Seth laughed, pinched the bum of a girl who came over to him and they went off together.

Flossie winked at me again and got up to go to the loo. Leaving Ben still sitting like a hypnotised floppy thing.

Charlie said, "Ah, is this some kind of girl plan?"

I said, "Noooooo."

Charlie said, "Oh God, it's a girl plan. Flossie likes Seth and Ben is her twit in a beanbag."

How did he know that?

Charlie said, "You're all naughty minxes. If it wasn't for the pull of your knees, I might storm off."

I said, "Oh, don't be cross because, well, don't be."

Charlie stretched back. "OK then, I'll give you a chance. But only because I like you."

Gosh, he made me feel all melty. And he did his lovely curly half-smile. I started making up a little rap song in my head about him, it went:

I'm a shrew
A shrew for you
I'm not in a funk
It's just that you are such a hunk.
Oh blimey
You're so finey
Pity you have a girl who's tiny.
Rastafari

Aye.

He said, "You're thinking, aren't you? I can always tell when you're thinking. So what are you thinking?"

I was thinking, *Don't mention the shrew thing.*

I said, "I was just thinking that some people can be, you know, tiny-ist."

Charlie looked puzzled and amused at the same time. "Neither of us know what you're talking about, do we?"

Then Charlie got up and said, "In a bit, crazy girl." And headed off into the crowd.

Well, I think if it's possible to change a quite good situation into a really useless one in one sentence, I have cornered the market.

Tiny-ist.

I had said tiny-ist.

CHAPTER 15
Naughty bumberskite

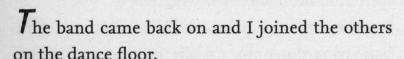

*T*he band came back on and I joined the others on the dance floor.

Cain was pacing about onstage as the band played a backbeat. He came to the microphone and said quietly into it, "This one's for someone who hasn't bin that well. She knows who she is. You might all know who she is."

And he deliberately looked across at the Bottomleys. Beverley was half smiling.

Cain said, "Yeah, it's called *Do you miss me – it's not mutual*."

And Seth and Ruben and Cain looked at each other and laughed. They are animals.

Vaisey shouted to me, "Jack said this one's about Beverley Bottomley and Jack said to Cain don't do it because she might kick off again."

The Bottomleys were all huddling round Beverley.

I couldn't see Charlie anywhere. So the Tree Sisters and me went and joined in the dancing circle.

Then Charlie came back and joined in, just opposite me. He smiled and gave me a thumbs-up. I soon forgot about the tiny-ist fiasco.

Vaisey did a spontaneous tribute dance when Jack did a drum solo. Then Jack stood up and bowed to her. Sweet.

And when the band rocked into *Get your coat on, girl, you're leaving*, Charlie and Phil leapt into the middle and started doing the twist.

Charlie shouted to me mid-twist, "Lullah, please, for me, for old times' sake. Do the unusual dancing."

The whole circle was chanting, "Lullah! Lullah!"

Oh no.

Oh yes.

I couldn't help myself, the excitement got the better of me. And I started hiddly diddlying before I knew what I was up to. My legs carried me into the centre of the ring and I did my bestiest Irish dancing.

It reminded me of when I was a little girl and my grandparents put me on the dining-room table to do Irish dancing for everyone. And Grandma said "Oh, she's so talented." And then Granddad said "Those are not normal legs" and then there was crying. And fighting.

When the song finished, Cain shouted into the microphone, "That's it. I've had enough. That's yer lot." And he kicked over Jack's drum kit.

Vaisey was beside herself. "He's kicked over Jack's drum kit."

The whole audience went mad, chanting, "One more song, one more song."

Bob scurried around onstage rebuilding the drum kit. The crowd wouldn't go home and kept chanting and eventually Cain came back to the microphone and said, "Awreet, this is the last one, and it's a slow one so you can all cop off to it."

Oh, he's so crude.

"It's called *I'm your darkest nightmare but it's me you want.*"

Jack began a really menacing drum beat. Vaisey whispered to me, "He's using his lucky sticks now."

Seth cranked out a jagged bass line and Cain growled out the lyrics with the mike right up against his mouth.

"Bad luck and trouble
Are my middle name
If you were me, you would be the same
Hey now, baby, why dun't you come with me
I want to show you how very bad I can be."

It was so weird and intense. I know what he's

talking about. He's talking about that kiss on the moors. In public.

I felt hot all over and stepped back so that I could hide behind the Tree Sisters, and almost fell into Charlie. He said, "Want to dance with me, Lullah?"

I said, "I don't think I could manage any more leaping."

Charlie smiled his lovely Charlie smile and said, "No, a proper dance with me."

And he put my arms up round his neck. And he put his arms round my waist. I couldn't help thinking about the hands on the bottom thing I'd talked to Vaisey about. But his hands felt nice on my back. And they seemed to be in the right position. And we danced.

He felt all lovely and warm against me. I could feel him breathing. And it was sort of magic as we drifted around in a slow circle. To the weird, slow singing of Cain. I'd never done slow dancing with a boy before.

I must have had my eyes closed because I

suddenly opened them to find I was facing the stage and Cain was looking directly at me. His dark eyes looked so angry and mean as he sang.

"Hey now, baby, why dun't you come with me
Because you know how very good things can be."

Then the song ended and Cain stormed off the stage shouting, "Now bog off."

Jack and Seth and Ruben took the applause.

Seth shouted to the crowd, "Treat us gently, girls!" And then they left the stage too.

Charlie stood with me for a minute and I didn't know what to do with my arms. He still had one of his round my waist and it felt lovely.

But then the lights went up and we sort of stepped apart.

Charlie said, "Er... thanks. That was nice. I'm just going to say well done to Jack. See you in a min."

I didn't know what had just happened. Charlie had danced with me like I was, well, a normal girl.

It had seemed quite romantic, I think. So what did 'see you in a min' mean?

People were putting their coats on. I could see Charlie with Jack and Vaisey hovering around. Jo and Phil were nowhere to be seen. Flossie had Ben by the shirt collar and was giving him little kisses on the mouth. He's almost sure to explode. I felt I should do something otherwise it looked like I was waiting for Charlie.

I turned to go to the loos, but found myself face to face with Beverley and her sisters. They chewed on their gum. They're not getting any smaller.

Eccles said, "Hello, you big long lanky posh bumberskite."

I felt very alone.

Beverley said, "I warned you to keep your hands off our lads."

As they were talking, the Tree Sisters had seen us and came over. Eccles said, "Ooooh, fear factor ten," in a really sarcastic way.

Beverley sneered, "Look at you, you great dunderwhelp. You think yer summat but you're nowt. You jumped-up tart. We dun't like you and your daft mates around here."

Jo said, "Er, why don't you call me daft again and see what happens next?"

Cain appeared between us tutting. "You know what Ted said, we're all little mates now, so play nicely, girls."

Beverley said to him, "We were awreet, me and you, before she turned up."

Cain said, "Beverley love, we were nivver awreet. You've been told there's nowt doing wi' me."

The whole of the crowd seemed to be waiting for a fight. Beverley suddenly burst into tears and ran out of the hall. Followed by Eccles, Dil and Chas. Eccles turned back to say to Cain as she went, "You're bloody evil, you."

He smiled and said, "Aye, it's a gift. Not many can pull it off, tha knows."

Eccles went off, shouting after her sisters, "Dun't let her head off to the stream!! She's got my bloody dress on."

Cain turned his attention to me. "Well, well,

those lasses seem not to like you. Especially that Beverley for some reason."

I held his gaze, but I wasn't going to speak to him. Everyone else was standing around, wondering if anything was going to kick off.

Cain said slowly but loudly, "Did you have a nice time with your garyboy mates then, Miss Tallulah? Dancing abaht."

I didn't say anything.

Cain went on. "Nowt to say to me, miss? I thought we were close. We have been close, haven't we? Reight close."

Some of the big lads sniggered.

I said, "Why don't you go off to your cave... and leave me alone."

Cain laughed, but not in a good way. He lowered his voice, but you could still hear every word. "But the last time, you didn't want me to go away, did you? That's not what you wanted at all."

The village lads were going, "Ooooooo! Naughty bumberskite."

Charlie appeared from out of the crowd and

stood in front of Cain with his arms folded and said, "Leave it out, mate."

Cain said, "Or what, big boy?"

Seth and Ruben came over and joined Cain. Then Phil, Ben and a couple of Woolfe boys joined Charlie. Jack was standing with Vaisey and he said, "Cain, leave it, mate."

Cain said softly, "Careful, posh lads, you don't want to get into any trouble with your mummies and daddies."

Phil said, "Er, I think you'll find that we're at Woolfe Academy because we are in trouble with our mummies and daddies."

Jo shouted, "Yeah, you lot, he tunnelled out of his last school AND he destroyed a rugby pitch."

I said, "OK, Jo, I think that's enough of..."

But Jo had really got into her stride now.

"They had to put a ball and chain on him to keep him at school."

Vaisey said reasonably, "Well, it was a rubber one but..."

Flossie said, "You're all talk and no action, you Hinchcliffs."

Seth said, "Oh, now then, you've really hurt our feelings, hasn't she, lads?"

And the Hinchcliff brothers nodded.

Flossie had gone a bit red. Seth walked right up to her, eyeball to – well, fringe. And he said, "Look at this big lass, she's not to be messed with, are you, love? She needs to be treated wi' respect."

And he smacked Flossie on the bum.

Oh dear.

Ben pushed back his fringe and went and stood in between Flossie and Seth. He said, "Look, leave my girlfriend alone. Go outside, Florence, I'll deal with this."

We all looked at Ben in amazement. Including Flossie.

So did Seth. For about ten seconds.

Then he got hold of Ben by his jacket and lifted him up and put him on a bar stool. He turned back to Flossie, "As I was saying…" And he took

Flossie's glasses off and kissed her on the mouth.

Then he gave her glasses back.

There was a moment's silence then Flossie went ballistic. She smacked him on the bum and kicked him.

While they were scuffling, Charlie said directly to Cain, "Listen, mate. It's just bad manners to harass girls who aren't interested in you. What is it with you Hinchcliffs? You've got your pick, why choose someone who doesn't like you? Tallulah said she doesn't want anything to do with you. She said so."

Ben had got off his stool and was wildly swinging at Seth who was holding him off with one hand.

Cain stopped laughing. He looked at Charlie and a hard, mean look came into his black eyes. Like coal shards gleaming.

He said slowly, "Doesn't want owt to do wi' me? Miss Tallulah doesn't want owt to do wi' me? You need to get your facts reight, MATE. Ask her about that time up on the moors, just me and her. She seemed to like me reight enough then."

Oh Holy Mother of God.

He went up close to Charlie.

"I dun't lie abaht lasses, I dun't need to, but I tell thee, she does want to do wi' me, otherwise why would she snog me? And it were a proper snog and I should know. If you don't believe me, ask the lady herself."

Oh Angel Gabriel and the Heavenly Back-up Team, please help me.

Charlie looked at me and said, "He's lying, isn't he, Lullah, and he's going to be sorry for lying."

Cain said, "Am I lying, Tallulah? Have we snogged?"

Oh no.

"Well. Erm. It's mostly lying because I was surprised and it was on the moors, it... Well, only... you know, accidentally and..."

Charlie looked angry.

He said, "So he's telling the truth?"

I put my head down and everyone near us

gasped, like I'd been found out as a witch.

Charlie said, "I see, well, I didn't know that."

Cain said, "There's a lot you dun't know, posh boy."

Charlie said, "Yeah – it seems so. I made a mistake."

And he gave me a horrible look. I wanted to say something, but I didn't know what.

Charlie walked over, grabbed his jacket and said to the other Woolfe boys, "See you. Don't forget the curfew."

And he looked me right in the eyes, just for a moment, like he hated me.

Maybe I should dash after him? But I didn't know what to say. Now he knew that I had snogged Cain. And so did the rest of Heckmondwhite.

Vaisey came and gave my hand a little squeeze.

Flossie was out of breath after tussling. She leaned against me, panting and said to Seth, "You big lug."

Seth said, "You know I like dirty talk. If you

get tired of floppy boy, I'll see you outside when we've packed up."

And he and Ruben went off backstage.

Cain looked into my eyes and said, "Well, well, what a to-do. Garyboy didn't seem reight pleased, did he? See you." And he went off backstage as well.

People were filing out of the hall into the moonlight. I had to get out into the fresh air. I felt faint. Some of the other Dother Hall girls crowded round me.

"What was all that about?"

"Is it true about you and Cain?"

"He's gorgeous, isn't he?"

"I'd snog him."

"Or that Charlie."

Vaisey slipped her arm through mine as we walked outside.

Flossie said, "I think if you like Cain even though he's bad, you should—"

I said, "I don't, I don't like him. I like Charlie and he hates me now."

Vaisey said, "No, he doesn't, he was just trying to look after you."

As they left for Dother Hall, Vaisey said to Flossie, "Aren't you going to wait for Seth, Flossie? He said he'd see you outside."

Flossie said, "Hell, no. That boy needs to learn some manners. Night, y'all."

Jo said, "Yeah, see you, Lullah. Everything will be all right. But boy, Charlie was mad though, wasn't he? He must have felt like a right idiot defending you and then finding out you were a secret Cain-snogger."

I let myself into Dandelion Cottage quietly. I could hear snoring and crept up the wooden stairs to my squirrel room.

What a night.

I didn't know which was the worst bit. Charlie being angry with me after we'd had our special slow dance or Cain being so sneering and mean.

And humiliating me in public.

Now everyone knows.

That night I had a weird dream.

I dreamed I was Kate in *Taming of the Shrew*, only I was half horsey, well, the leggy parts. And I was cantering about, kicking stuff with my horsey legs.

And Charlie appeared in a white frilly shirt and jodhpurs. He said, "It's all right, Kate, I've got a big shrew and it's got your name written all over it." And he showed me the shrew and it had 'Kate' written on it in black felt tip.

He said, "Let's eat it together."

And he put one end of the shrew in my mouth and the other end in his mouth. And we both started crunching. It was quite a crunchy shrew.

Then Cain appeared in a Cavalier's hat and black mask like a highwayman. He got his sword out and chopped the shrew in half so that Charlie was left with half a shrew in his mouth.

But it wasn't dead – it was just looking at me with its little beady eyes.

Then it winked.

Chapter 16
The church bells of doom

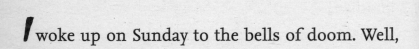

I woke up on Sunday to the bells of doom. Well, the church bells.

The Dobbins looked in on me on their way to church but I pretended to be asleep. It was cosy in my squirrel bed and maybe, if I stayed in it for the rest of my life, no one could get me. No one could humiliate me when I was safe in my...

There was a stomping up the stairs and Ruby clattered through the door with Matilda. She got into bed with me and shouted, "Boy, are you an IDIOT!"

She still had her coat and boots on. I said, "How do you know?"

She said, "Everyone knows. They'll probably mention it in church. So tell me the details."

I told her, and she looked at me with her mouth open.

"Well I'll go to the bottom of our stairs. So let me get this, you tongue-tangled with Cain. And you nivver said. And Cain told in front of everybody and Charlie got the hump. Boy are you an idiot."

I said, "You've said that already."

She said, "Yeah but you're a double idiot. Have a jelly bean."

Actually, it was a relief to talk to Rubes. I said, "I'll have to leave Dother Hall."

Ruby was sucking her jelly bean to get it as small as it would go, but she said, "Dun't worry, nobody's that bothered. I bet no one will mention it, it'll be old news by now."

Yeah, she's probably got a point. Who's going to be bothered about what Cain says?

An hour later, we heard the door open downstairs and Dibdobs shouted up, "Hellllooooooo, it's us, we're back!"

I shouted, "Hello!"

And Ruby said, "'Ello, I'm here as well."

Dibdobs shouted, "Hello, Ruby!"

And the twins shouted, "Hello, Booby!"

Ten minutes later Dibdobs came up with tea and toast. She put it on the bed and beamed at me.

As she went out she said, "Well, you need to build your strength up, Lullah, if you're going out canoodling with boys."

Oh dear God, she knows.

Everyone knows.

I said to Ruby, "I'll have to stay in bed forever. I can't face people."

Ruby got up and said, "Look, this is the North. People here dun't even wear vests in winter. One of the lads in The Iron Pies wore a short-sleeved T-shirt all last December and he's the snowplough man. He's got Northern grit. You've got to get Northern grit."

I've spent the whole afternoon pulling myself together and making notes about Northern grit.

Right, this is my list.

1. *Walk tall. Straighten my shoulders and look people in the eye. So what if I've snogged a boy, it's not a hanging offence (p.s. although it may be a 'sitting on' offence if I bump into Beverley Bottomley).*
2. *If in doubt, look 'hard' and shrug. Or else try a distant smile.*
3. *Never complain about the cold.*
4. *Wear more hats.*

I've been practising my special 'Northern grit' attitude ready for tomorrow. I'm going to tie my hair back in a ponytail and adopt a nonchalant shrug and wear a hat. I think shrugging is the way forward. Anyway, I haven't really done anything to be ashamed of.

Well, I have actually. But onwards and upwards.

Also, as an added precaution, I'm going to set off slightly earlier tomorrow so that I don't bump into anyone in the village. I'll be old news by the time I get to Dother Hall.

Besides this week will be hectic because it's the assessment performances on Friday lunchtime.

It's all very well having Northern grit lists – but when I woke up in the middle of the night I couldn't help remembering Charlie's face. The look he gave me as he left. And I can't bear it that he really hates me because... well... I...

And then the tears started.

And once they had, I couldn't stop. I muffled my face in my pillow and really cried.

I must have cried myself to sleep.

My eyes were quite swollen when I woke up. But I did cold water splashing to perk them up. When I walked into the entrance hall, I was besieged by girls. Nearly everyone asked me if it was true that I was a Cain-snogger. And, what was worse, they seemed to think it was a good thing to be.

Even Lav.

Oh God.

She came swishing and blinking up and ruffled my hair.

"To be sure, Lullah, you are the dark horse now, aren't you? All this kissing the boys! And the naughty boys!"

I tried Number 1 and 3 on my Northern grit list. I straightened my shoulders and said, "This cold's quite bracing, isn't it?"

Vaisey and I are planning to rehearse every lunchtime in any space we can find for our duet performance. I thought if I plunged myself into work I could forget about Charlie. And about my new reputation at Dother Hall as a sort of groupie for The Jones.

At our first rehearsal for the assessment, Vaisey said, "Even though Jack will never see this piece, I'm still doing it for him in a way. I want to do what he said. You know, show my true self to the world."

So we trotted around in the dance studio working out our moves.

Vaisey said, "I think Black Beauty and Merrylegs are symbolic of my feelings as a child about friendship and loss. I loved my pony Goldie, but then I got too big for her and she got sold and I cried for two weeks."

I didn't say anything.

Vaisey said, "Do you know what I mean, Lulles?"

Oh yes, I knew all about the crying game.

The shame game.

The pain game.

It's all the same game.

But, as Sidone says, the show must go on.

Vaisey was trying out some dressage moves for Black Beauty when I reminded her of the rap I'd written about the owlets.

She said, "Wow, that's a brilliant idea. A rap. You could do a rap in this piece. Do you think you could make one up now?"

I said, "I'll have a go. I'll just improvise…"

I grabbed the false horsey legs and banged one of the hoofs against the radiator. It made a nice clunky sound. So I started stalking around, using the hoofs to bang things as I rapped.

"Yeah, me know about the crying game,
The crying game is my game.
And me know about shame.
And the blame
It's my middle name
Aye
Peace."

Vaisey said, "Wow, that's really cool, isn't it? It's brilliant. Merrylegs could sing it right at the end as he dies. Honestly, Lulles, I don't think there's going to be a dry eye in the house."

I didn't say, but personally I think that a horse doing a rap song would mean there wouldn't be a dry seat in the house.

Oh noooo, I can feel another enormous embarrassing incident coming on.

It happened even sooner than I thought. As Vaisey was prancing about neighing, she said, "This is the bit where we're happy and free in our field playing together. I'll do the cross hoof thing and you do high prancing and whinnying."

Just then, Dr Lightowler popped her beak round the door and began to watch.

At the end she said, "Excellent, Vaisey. Your performance has depth and pathos and your singing is a delight. And Tallulah, well, what can I say that I haven't said before?"

And she looked unblinkingly at me.

At least she wasn't winking.

As she went out, I shouted, "Oh yeah, Beaky. Wait till you hear my rap."

Actually, I didn't shout that because I didn't want my head pecked off.

But Vaisey thought I was brilliant. She said, "I think this is gonna be great, Lullah. Nobody's ever going to forget this performance."

When the other Tree Sisters went to singing practice, I went to sit in a lavatory by myself just for a little break from having Northern grit. But I couldn't even get in the loo because there was a notice from Bob on it.

> **Listen up, dudes.**
> **Appliance out of action.**
> **Bad scene with a vole.**
> **On it.**
> **Bob (The Iron Pies' next gig is in Follyfoot. Be there. Or not be there.)**

By Wednesday the Tree Sisters were all getting boy withdrawal. No one has heard anything from the

Woolfe boys since the gig. They haven't appeared at our Special Tree.

I'm a bit worried that Charlie has said horrid things about me to the other lads. I don't think he would because he's so nice. But he was very angry.

At lunchtime, I found Jo snogging a mirror in the loos.

I said, "Now you're being extra weird."

Jo said, "Am I? Am I? Well, you snog me then."

I said, "What are you talking about?"

She looked at me. "If you were a Samaritan and I was starving, would you pass by on the other side of the road?"

"Er, no, but you're not starving and..."

She said, "It's the same thing. Snogging is as essential as food. I've got snogging withdrawal. It's like I had a big fat snog meal on Saturday, and then I've not even had a snog snack since. So why is it so very hard for you to snog me in my hour of need?"

I couldn't say anything. I could only look at her in amazement.

She stormed out. "Right, if you won't help me, it'll have to be teddy."

Who's Teddy?

When I got to college on Thursday, Vaisey was on the front doorstep hopping and bobbling around in a frenzy of curls. "Look, Lullah, look!" And she held out a piece of paper. "It's a note from Jack. He left it under our Special Tree."

I felt a bit apprehensive. "Did he, erm, say anything about Charlie, or, or me or anything?"

Vaisey's note was mostly drawings of fingering positions on guitar frets. She kissed the letter. "Isn't it romantic?"

Then Jo burst through the door with her teddy. She said, "Have you met my new boyfriend? He's called Little Ted."

This is turning into a theatrical lunatic asylum.

It's horrid having Charlie not liking me. I don't think I can bear it. If only he would talk to me.

And it's all because of Cain. Who couldn't care

less about me, he just likes making trouble for people. He said those things about the kissing just to humiliate me.

In a way I suppose he must hate me as well. And Dr Lightowler certainly one thousand per cent and a half hates me.

What makes me especially hateful?

It reminds me of that song that Cain sang at the gig. What did he say?

Bad luck and trouble
Are my only friends.
I've been down since I began to crawl
If it wasn't for bad luck,
I wouldn't have no luck at all.

That's me. My life is over.

At afternoon break, Gudrun bobbed into Monty's reading forum and said, "Vaisey, Jo, Flossie and Lullah, there's a telephone call for you, in Sidone's office."

What?

Flossie said, "Ah, it'll be Hollywood calling, dahlings, they've heard about my tights juggling."

Sidone was on the phone when we went in. Wearing a feather boa. She was talking to someone and saying, "Darling, darling, they're here. Give my regards to Tinseltown. *Ciao!*"

She cradled the receiver to her bosom. "It's our golden girl, Honey!"

Flossie reached for the phone and said, "It *is* Hollywood calling!"

Sidone was gripping the receiver. "We've had a lovely chat. So many memories came rushing back. I don't know if I've mentioned that I had a small part in 2001: *A Space Odyssey*. I was flown over for the filming and I remember I had my fur bikini made at a costumier in downtown Hollywood. Now what was the name...?"

We all stared at her, thinking, *Come on, give us the bloody phone!!!*

At last she handed it over and we all put our ears near.

We heard Honey's voice, "Itth me!!!!"

Sidone said, "You've got all break to speak to the dear girl. I'll be back after."

We shouted down the phone at the same time.

"We love you!"

"I miss you."

"Is it hot?"

"Phil broke into the dorm and fell through the potting shed."

"Bob's joined The Iron Pies!"

"Dr Lightowler hates me!"

"Seth snogged me!"

Until, in a pause, we heard her say, "Thpeak thloly! And one at a time tho I can hear you."

Flossie shoved us aside and grabbed the phone. She said, "Seth snogged me!" Do you remember the Hinchcliffs? And Lullah let Cain snog her. On the moors!"

We could hear Honey laughing as we crowded near the receiver.

"I have my vewy own thervant boy. He getth me things. Itth nithe."

Jo said, "What, is he sort of like Bob?"

Honey giggled. "Ith Bob weawing thpeedos?"

Urgh, what a thought!

She told us about her screen tests, and that she has a little part in a film called *Madame Gigi's School of Love*. She's having such a great time. It seems a long way from playing Merrylegs at falling down Dother Hall.

Her film is about Madame Gigi teaching about boys and how to get what you want from them. And how to teach them to snog properly. And how to train boys. Wow.

She said, "The good thing ith, itth only a film, but it weally workth. I have thwee boyfwends awready on the go and they're coming along nithely. One'th got blond hair, he'th a thurfer, one'th got dark hair, he'th a muthician, and one'th ginger."

I said, "Is he a biscuit?"

Which made her laugh.

Vaisey said, "So what's Madame Gigi's best advice?"

Then the bell rang for the end of break.

Jo said, "Yeah, quick, give us one thing."

Honey was quiet then she lisped, "The motht impowtant thing with boyth ith to tell the twuth about what you want."

Blimey.

That's great advice, except if I tell the truth about what I want, I don't get it. Also I don't know what the truth is. Or who to tell it to.

Sidone came back then to tell us time was up.

We said goodbye and Honey said, "Itth lovely here and evewyone ith lovely, but I mith my Twee Thithteth more than anything."

We all had a little bit of a cry then.

Back in my squirrel room that night. I told Dibdobs I was studying *The Taming of the Shrew* for homework and went to bed early.

I was wondering about what Honey said about telling boys what you want. Is it really all right to do that? And what if they say no?

There was a knocking at the bottom of my door. Oh no.

A little voice said, "Ug oo."

The lunatic twins.

Ah well, in their own strange boy way they do seem to love me. I opened the door. There they were, Sam and Max sucking on their dodies with Micky and Dicky under their arms.

Dibdobs came bobbing along from the boys' room. "Lullah, the boys and Micky and Dicky wanted to say nighty-night."

I said nighty-night and shut my door as they went off to their bedroom. I could hear her explaining things to the boys, "Lullah has to go to beddy-byes now because she's doing a play at big school."

Sam said, "Big pool."

Dibdobs was chattering on. "Yes, it's called *The Taming of the Shrew*. That's a funny name, isn't it, boys? Can you say *The Taming of the Shrew*?"

Max said, "Tamin' of the shoe."

Dibdobs laughed. "No, darling, it's a SHREW."

Sam shouted, "It's a SHOE!!!!!"

When I had my breakfast the next day, Dibdobs looked a bit tired. The twins came in and looked at me and then handed me a shoebox. Max said, "SHOE house."

Dibdobs shouted, "Boys, boys, I've explained to you a lot, haven't I? It's not a shoe, it's a SHREW."

Max and Sam nodded and repeated, "Not a shoe, it's a SHOE!!!"

CHAPTER 17
Should I put nail varnish on my hoofs?

*P*erformance lunchtime day. Still no news about Charlie. Ah well. That's it.

It's been a week, he does officially hate me.

Perhaps if I see him in Heckmondwhite over the weekend, I could explain things to him. I don't know how, as I can't even explain things to me.

And I'm me.

There's been no sign of Cain either.

Maybe he just hides in the moors and only

comes out when he knows he has an opportunity to ruin my life.

At midday, everyone doing the lunchtime performance went to the main hall to get ready. Backstage was full of excited mad girls all looking forward to the performance.

Apart from me.

You know when something is so terrible that you think it can't be true and won't ever happen? That's what a performance assessment is like when you're wearing home-made horse legs. Which are actually stuffed tights. And have papier mâché hoofs stuck on the end. And you've got false furry ears on.

If ever there was a time for Northern grit, this was it. Anyway the worst has already happened to me. I said to Vaisey and the girls backstage, "Oh well, as James Bond said, 'You only die once.'"

Flossie said, "Er, I think you'll find he said, 'You only live twice.'"

Vaisey said, "I can hear men's voices."

Oh God, Monty must have asked Biffo and Sprogsy along. Better and better.

Sidone came backstage to see us. She was wearing a tiara and a lot of make-up. She was thrilled. "Girls, my girls, I've just come back to say 'break a leg' to you all. Well, in Vaisey's and Tallulah's case, I should say 'legs'."

She tinkled with laughter. She hadn't finished though. "As a special surprise, I've asked the headmaster of Woolfe Academy to join us with some guests for our show. He is most keen on the arts and is talking of perhaps investing in Dother Hall. He thinks that girls have a civilising effect on his boys."

Flossie snorted after she'd gone. "Why would we want to have a civilising effect on boys?? I want them goddam young men to go ape wild!!!"

Jo looked through a slit in the curtains and said, "Oh my God, all of Woolfe Academy are here."

It couldn't be true!

I said, "No, no, nooooooo… Can you see Charlie?"

Jo said, "Yeah and Phil and Ben too and there's Jack, right at the front."

I said to Vaisey, "Did you know about this?"

She looked ashen-faced.

"No, no, I didn't. I... Jack didn't say anything about it in his note. He just said he'd learned a new fret sequence. Oh, Lullah, I can't go on. I'm not going on, not in these legs and doing the horsey dancing and everything. I can't. We've only got to Number 5 on your Lulu-luuuve List. I'll have to pretend I'm sick. I AM sick. Let's say we're sick."

She was trembling all over.

I said, "Sidone's just seen us, she'll know we're not sick."

Vaisey said, "Well, I'm not doing it." And she started taking off her false ears.

Jo said, "Oh, come on, Vaisey, put your ears back on. We're pros, darling. The show must go on."

I said, "It's all very well for you, you're just singing and swanning about."

Jo said, "Yeah, I know. Have I got enough lipstick on?"

I said, "I don't know, should I have put nail varnish on my hoofs???"

I think I was about to have a hysterical fit.

Flossie said, "Well, I'm juggling my tights, you know."

Vaisey was shaking her head from side to side, moaning, "I can't, I just can't. I want him to think I'm pretty and..."

Flossie said, "AND you'll fail your assessment if you don't."

Vaisey looked like she was about to cry.

It's different for me. I haven't any pride left. Shame, after all, is my middle name. But Vaisey will feel terrible if she fails.

I made a decision. It's Number 3 on the Northern grit list. I put one of my front legs round her shoulder and said, "Look, little pal, Jack will like you whatever you do so, come on, let's do this for Black Beauty and Merrylegs and friendship."

Jo said, "Would you go out there, Lullah, in front of Charlie and all the lads? Really?"

I said, "Yeah, so what if Charlie's here? He hates me anyway. But there are people out there waiting to see us. People who love the theatre, people who we let our feet bleed for. People who are waiting to give us our golden slippers of applause."

Vaisey gripped my hoof and Jo said, "When you get the golden slippers of applause, don't forget to ask for four… each."

Vaisey put her ears back on. "Lullah, we'll do it for each other!"

Flossie and Jo clapped us on the back.

We were on fourth after Honsy and Natasha. The Black Beauty music began and Sidone announced, "Tallulah and Vaisey bring us the joy and sadness of a two-horse friendship."

It was the longest five minutes of my life.

We trotted on lightly as foals, we nuzzled, we jumped, we pulled toy carts about. I strummed on a guitar and Black Beauty played the harmonica as I sang my rap song. Finally and slowly I died in Black Beauty's legs.

I died to the sound of gales of laughter.

Backstage, Vaisey gave me a big hug and said, "You are truly a great pal. I never would've done that without you and now I feel so good. People really liked it, didn't they? They clapped, didn't they? It was a shame they laughed when you died though. Maybe they thought you were just pretending?"

Flossie said, "Mr Barraclough had to be helped out he was laughing so much."

When I'd taken my legs and ears off, I thought I'd just go off quietly and see if I could creep away down the lane, go home and get immediately into my bed. Forever.

No one would notice me leaving because everyone was too busy flirting with everyone else. The boys of Woolfe Academy were everywhere, talking to the girls, Sidone was flirting with Hoppy the headmaster, so was Monty, and Blaise had cornered some terrified little bloke in a tracksuit.

The worst thing was knowing that Charlie had seen me. If he didn't already think I was an out-and-out twit of the first water, he would now.

Vaisey had ripped off her legs and went to find Jack, and Jo didn't even bother to go round the back of the hall. She just went through the curtains and leapt off the stage on to Phil's lap.

I crept down the back corridor and got my coat from the cloakroom without bumping into anyone. Oh, I was miserable.

I mean, it's nice to make people laugh, but is that all I can do?

I stepped outside. Oh good, it was raining. As I put my coat collar up, I heard someone say, "Lullah, that was, that was, well, I don't know what that was, but it was a gem!"

Charlie was there in the doorway.

I couldn't bear any more of being the fool. But it wasn't Charlie's fault. And also it was nice that he wasn't being mean to me after what had happened. He smiled at me. So I tried to smile at him a bit. I couldn't get any words out, but I managed the smile.

He said, "Where are you going?"

I gulped and said in a cheery voice, "Oh, I've just got a bit of foraging to do at... home."

Charlie said, "Are you upset, Tallulah?"

I said, "No."

He went on. "Vaisey said you didn't know we were all going to be here and that you didn't want to look stupid, but that you did it for her."

I felt my eyes fill with tears.

He cleared his throat and said, "This is becoming a bit of a theme, isn't it, between me and you? Me being a prat and having to apologise."

What did he mean? Was he apologising for laughing at me?

I said, "Well, you know, I suppose a horse doing a rap song is quite funny really."

Charlie laughed again and said, "Well, it's more than funny, it's... but that's not what I mean. I mean about the other night at the gig. Kicking off about you and Cain. When it's none of my business."

I said, "I... well... he..."

Charlie went on. "Lullah, you don't have to say

anything. I had no right to do it. And I'm sorry. And the Cain thing, I mean, that's your business. I just don't think he's a nice guy and I didn't want him to be mean to you. And in public as well. That's all. So I'm sorry for being a prat. You can kick me with your hoof if you like."

I looked at him.

He said, "Go on, you might like it."

I kicked his ankle and I smiled.

He said, "By the way, keep rapping. I think you've got a nice voice. Maybe ease up on the Rastafarian vibe though."

He looked like he was about to say something else, but then he spotted a prefect coming his way and had to go back in.

I'm so happy that we're friends again. In fact, I made up a little spontaneous song. Charlie said I had a nice voice. Maybe I'll become a singer songwriter. My song is called *Charlie* and it goes like this:

He likes me
He likes me
He really, really likes me.
Yaroooooooooooooooooooooooo.

Maybe not a chart-topper.

I was exhausted when I got back to the cottage and frozen. Dibdobs gave me tea in front of the blazing fire. She's made me some fir-cone earrings and sprayed them gold. I had to try them on for her while the twins stared at me as if I was a very early Father Christmas. In earrings. Dibdobs thought they looked a treat and started her spontaneous hugging.

"Oh, oh, Lullah, you look so beautiful, like a princess. With your black hair and those green eyes, oh, oh."

And she actually started crying. And hugging.

This was new. And sweet. Until the twins joined in with Micky and Dicky.

Later, when I was tucked up in my bed, the twins came in with 'the shoe'. "For seepin'," as Max told me.

Dibdobs came in to collect it because it has to go in its box. She said, "I'm so sorry, Lullah, the boys are treating it like a pet. I must find a real shrew to show them."

Thinking about shrews made me think of the owlets. It's so windy and wild outside. I hope they've got better at hunting. I wonder if Cain still looks out for them like he used to when they were tiny. It was one of the only good things about him.

Ooooh, I'm so tired, what a day. But now I've done this thing for Vaisey I can put my horsey legs behind me for good.

As I drifted off to sleep, I thought, *Charlie likes me. Even though he knows all about the Cain thing.*

CHAPTER 18
The Dark Black Crow of Heckmondwhite

When I went into Dother Hall on Monday morning, there was an enormous owl waiting on the doorstep. Wearing glasses.

Is it my imagination or are Dr Lightowler's glasses getting bigger?

She said, "I've been thinking about you all weekend."

I smiled and said, "Oh, that's nice, I—"

"Tallulah Casey, yet again you choose to drag

the reputation of Dother Hall through the mud."

What? She couldn't have heard about the Cain thing surely. Could she?

She went on. "At a PUBLIC event with the eyes of the world upon us, when we need our neighbours to support us, you deliberately do your silly, childish antics in front of invited guests. Everything is SOOOOOO funny to you, isn't it? Anything for a cheap laugh."

Oh, she meant the lunchtime performance thing. I tried to tell her, "But it was all Vaisey's idea, she..."

Dr Lightowler shook her feathers, I mean, cloak. "Don't try and blame others. I've always known what you are. You're a selfish girl."

I blinked in amazement. What was she talking about?

"And worst of all, untalented. Don't think I didn't understand your so-called rap about 'owls'. Well, you've bitten off more than you can chew this time, my girl."

She swished off, turning her head round every

now and then to look at me. Before she swept into her eyrie.

Throughout the day, every time I came out of a door it seemed that Dr Lightowler was there looking at me. Not blinking and then twitching. I said to the others, "I'd better not wear anything brown, she might think I'm a shrew."

I'm trying to make a joke about it, but it's not nice.

At break, I got a message to go and see Sidone.

When I went into her office, she was lying on her chaise longue in harem trousers, smoking a hubbly-bubbly. She said, "I know it's a filthy habit, but I picked it up in Marrakesh when we were on tour with *Carry on Matron* and well... that's another story. Pull up some cushions."

I piled up some cushions and sat on the floor at her feet.

"So, Miss Casey, you had a chequered beginning with us here at Dother Hall, and to be quite truthful it was only because Ms Fox says you are an extraordinary presence and bound to be quite tall that we kept you on. Not everyone thought it a good idea. This is a hard business and in order to survive you have to be skilful. Dr Lightowler specially came to talk to me about your lunchtime performance."

Oh no. She'd actually done it.

Sidone adjusted her turban.

"Dr Lightowler says that she thinks that you have a great talent for broad comedy."

What? Great talent?

Had I misjudged Owly?

Sidone continued, "Yes, we had an interesting chat. She reminded me of when you were the horse in the Mummers play at The Blind Pig, and then your hilarious horse in *A Midsummer Night's Dream*. And, of course, your duet on Friday. Merrylegs, wasn't it? I don't know why it hadn't struck me before. Until Dr Lightowler pointed it out, I'd forgotten how fond you are of the 'horse genre'."

The Horse Genre?

Sidone puffed on her hubbly-bubbly. "As Mr de Courcy often says about a career in the thea-tah, 'she is a harsh mistress'."

I said, "Yes, well, I was thinking about, you know, specialising in comedy. Ms Fox thought—"

Sidone's head was lost in a cloud of smoke, but I could still hear her. "So Dr Lightowler suggested you should consider specialising in horse work. She thinks you have the legs for it. And, of course, it's regular work, especially at Christmas with the pantos, and then there's always children's theatre groups. Little children love a horse."

When I came out of her study, I felt like I had been hit on the head with a mallet. I was so dazed. It had come to this. A life as a pantomime horse.

I didn't tell the girls what had gone on in Sidone's study. I just said that it was a general chat about careers. But the Tree Sisters kept on asking me why Sidone wanted to see just me and not them. All day they went on.

In the end, I went and hid in the 'vole lavatory' and sat on the seat which was all taped down. Flossie climbed on the seat of the next-door loo and popped her head over the partition. I heard her and looked up, and she said "Goddammit, Miss Lullabelle, tell us why you gotta face like a baby's smacked bum. What in tarnation did Ms Beaver say?"

Eventually, I told the Tree Sisters about the panto horse thing. There was silence from them at first and then they laughed for about a year. I felt even more stupid and lonely.

The bell rang for last period and we had to go to Monty's reading class.

I cannot believe he's reading *War Horse* to us. He says it's for the "interesting narrative perspective", but they have puppet horses in the play, don't they? Has he been talking to Dr Lightowler?

Vaisey whispered to me, "Come to the dorm at the end of the day for a special emergency Tree Sisters' meeting. To be held in Flossie's bed for warmsies."

After the final bell, as we went up the stairs, Vaisey gave me a hug and said, "Don't worry, your sisters won't let you down. I'll help you like you helped me."

It was freezing in the dorm and the tarpaulin roof was flapping. We all got into Flossie's bed and Jo said, "Funnily enough, when I was Bob's assistant, we fixed this bed. There were some dodgy wooden slats and he used a prototype slat made out of glue, newspaper and..."

At which point the whole bed collapsed, and we had to go into Vaisey's bed.

Vaisey said, "You didn't fix this one as well, did you?"

When we'd bounced up and down and found that the bed didn't collapse, we settled down again. The Tree Sisters gave me a pep talk. I had to write the main points down to put in my Darkly Demanding Damson Diary later so I wouldn't forget.

The main points are:

1. *Dr Lightowler is mad.*
2. *As a snake.*
3. *But even madder.*
4. *So get over it.*

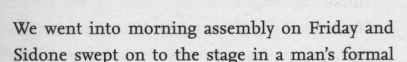

We went into morning assembly on Friday and Sidone swept on to the stage in a man's formal evening suit.

"Be careful what you dream of, my girls! Such excitements. Such joyful news!! Sound out the bells!"

Then she waited and said again, "Sound out the bells!"

Gudrun was on the side of the stage with her gong. Gradually she seemed to notice the silence. Especially as Sidone was holding her arms out towards her. She struck her gong.

Sidone came to the front of the stage and began. "Mr Legge..."

Gudrun sounded her gong again.

Sidone said, "Thank you, thank you Gudrun, enough. Mr Legge has just telephoned with a marvellous, a simply inspired idea."

We looked at each other. Jo said quietly, "Who is this Mr Legge when he's at home?"

We shrugged.

Sidone continued.

"Yes, girls. Last Friday, when Mr Legge brought his young men to our humble artistic temple to see our lunchtime performances, he was so impressed."

Oh, now we got it. She meant Hoppy!!!

I whispered to the others, "You see what this means – we've struck comedy gold. Hoppy, who has only got one leg, is actually called Mr Legge. Please, please tell me that his first name is Arthur. Then he could be Mr A. Legge. Or if he's a Cockney... Arf-a-legge!!!"

Sidone was still going on.

"Yes, Mr Legge was so impressed, he wants us to have a 'coming together' in the woods that divide us."

Everyone cheered. Jo shouted out, "Like a sort of love-in, Ms Beaver?"

Sidone trilled, "Perhaps, perhaps Jo. Music, dance, a winter feast. Songs, verse, performances from *The Taming of the Shrew*, fire and food. The crackling of a bonfire among the dark trees; a beacon of art and joy in the bleak midwinter. A feast for the eyes and nourishment for the soul."

Good heavens.

I said to the Tree Sisters as we left the hall, "You know what this is, don't you? It's a big bonfire with snacks and us prancing around like fools and Mr Barraclough laughing at me again. It's the Taming of the Tights."

Flossie gathered us into an enormous Tree Sister hug. "Yes, that's true, but you're missing out the most interesting thing. There will be many, MANY boys there."

Everyone at college seemed very merry about the planned Taming of the Tights. Ms Fox said, "Well, sensation seekers, this may save our bacon. Few quid from Woolfe Academy and we'll be laughing!"

Monty was skipping about when we went for our afternoon session. Clutching his heart and saying, "We must have 'enthusiasm', girls, do you know what that means?"

Jo put her hand up. "Like when someone says, 'Would you like a Jazzle?' And you say, 'Not half, matey!!!'"

Flossie said, "Or someone offers to carry you around instead of you having to walk everywhere and you say, 'Yes sirree Bob!'"

Everyone started yelling out stuff and Monty had to shout over the top. "Good ideas, girls, but enthusiasm – from the Greek *enthousiasmos* – means literally to have the god within! To fill yourself to the brim with life. As Sprogsy shouted that night in Rome as we were running from the police, 'Breathe, eat, drink, life!!!' Try it in your own lives. Whatever you do, do it with *ENTHOUSIASMOS!!!*"

Monty's lecture on enthusiasm might be the worst thing he has ever done in his long career of doing the worst thing. Since his class we've been doing everything with enthusiasm. And I do mean everything. In the café, Flossie shouted at the dinner lady who asked her what kind of crisps she wanted, "I want the FINEST Corkers known to humanity!!!"

The Tree Sisters carried the 'enthusiasm' theme into my nightly pep talk.

Flossie started. "Here are some major plus points of your life, Lullah. We've written them down and you must absorb them."

Jo said, "When we say 'absorb', we mean 'eat'."

I said, "Is this because Monty said we must 'breathe, eat and drink life'?"

Jo said, "Yes."

I said, "He didn't mean eat everything surely?"

Flossie said, "Shall we get on? Not seeing boys makes me a bit bad-tempered and violent."

I read my major plus points list.

1. The Tree Sisters love you!
2. Blaise loves you!
3. Gudrun, Bob, Sidone and Monty love you in their own way! (Which is of course not what everyone would want, but nevertheless you have got it. Big time.)
4. Ruby loves you! And Matilda is mental about you!
5. The Dobbins are mad about you. And also just mad.
6. The twins adore you.
7. The owlets love you, they just can't be bothered coming to see you.
8. Phil, Ben, Jack and Charlie like you! (Which actually, in Charlie's case, seeing what happened to him, is pretty good.)

Flossie said, "So, as you see, that is a lot of liking-ness for one person. We haven't even put down the maybe-like-you people, you know, your parents, brother etc."

Jo said, "Yes, so quickly, quickly, eat your list with *enthousiasmos*."

As they watched me chewing my list, I was thinking, *Yes, but does Charlie like me? He said he did, but that was ages ago.*

Still it was nice to be with the Tree Sisters. And I'm very happy that they care about me.

Vaisey said, "And Lullah, the Taming of the Tights can be when you really show Dr Lightowler what you can do."

I spat my list out when I walked home. I had stored it in my cheek like a hamster.

Saturday, miraculously, was nice and sunny. I woke up feeling chirpy for the first time in days. Whatever Dr Lightowler said, other people thought I was clever and talented. My Tree Sisters loved me and that's the best thing that has ever happened to me. I have made my own little family.

I thought it was a good day to go owlet-seeking with Rubes. I went to call for Ruby and Mr Barraclough answered the door. His face brightened when he saw it was me. He said, "Hello, young man, at a bit of a loose end? Or are you miming? Is that it? Are you doing miming now?"

I said, "Mr Barraclough, is Ruby in?"

He said, "Ruby's taken Matilda to dog-dancing class in Little Waddle."

Was he joking? I could never tell.

I said, "I didn't know Matilda could do dog dancing."

Mr Barraclough said, "She can't, son, she's hopeless, but needs must when the devil drives. As a theatrical type yourself and a sensible young man of the world, you'll realise that you have to appeal to your market.

"Most of The Iron Pies' audience are of course hell-raisers and decadents like myself, but there are a few family types with little uns. Little uns who might like to see a doggie dancing. So we thought Matilda can earn her keep instead of generally lying around snoozing behind the drum kit."

Ruby's not going to be back until four so I went

off for a little wander by myself.

I might as well have a look in the barn. You never know, the owlets might still remember it and go back there. I haven't seen them since Lullah fell off my window sill.

It was nice out but windy. I took my hat off. I liked the feel of the wind tossing my hair around. Then it blew completely over my eyes so that I couldn't see where I was going.

And then my hair blew back again and I saw, on the path, Cain with his dog.

The Divil Himself.

The wind had blown his fringe down over his eyes and he had a black leather coat on with the collar turned up and leather gloves.

I felt my heart lurch.

The air around him seemed charged with energy. He wasn't moving, just standing there looking at me.

I couldn't turn round and go back home. Anyway, why should I? I'll walk straight past him with Northern grit Number 1.

He was still looking at me from under his eyelashes. Then, without looking away, he made a chucking noise with his teeth. Was he chucking at me?

How rude.

But then from the branch above him a feathery bombshell flew down on to his outstretched glove and then another one. Owlets!!! It was little Lullah and little Ruby! I forgot about him and ran up to see them. They were tugging at something he was holding in his glove.

I said, "Oh, oh, it's them. What are you feeding them?"

He looked up at me with his dark eyes and held mine for a moment then cast his gaze down to the owlets. "Baby shrews."

He was an animal!

The owlets gulped the baby shrews down. They looked like they were smiling all the time they were doing it. They probably were.

It reminded me of my dream about being a shrew and Dr Lightowler looking at me, ready to eat me. But they weren't like Dr Lightowler, they were my children. My wild children.

I couldn't help myself. I went nearer to them and said softly, "It's me, big Lullah, hellloooooooo."

Fortunately, I remembered not to fluff myself up or do the blinky-eye thing. They looked at me and cheeped. It made me want to burst into tears with love. And now they were doing head-swivelling!! For me, they were swivelling their heads for me. No one has ever swivelled their head for me. I put my finger out and touched each of their tiny feathery chests. They cheeped again as the shrew tails disappeared into their beaks.

Then Cain shook his glove and said, "Get gone now, you two lazy arses, get hunting."

Both of them plummeted to the ground, took a few staggering steps and then careened off into the air.

I shouted after them, "See you soon! Come back to the barn, I'll bring snacks!"

For the first time Cain smiled his crooked, mean smile. "Bloody hell, tha's barmier than I remember, soft lass."

I was determined to hold my ground. Then he licked his lips and leaned back against the fence, crossing his arms and putting one leg over the other.

Holy moly.

I couldn't stand the silence so I babbled, "Why are you, with, are they... I mean, do you see them often?"

He said languidly, "There's nowt in it, we're just good friends."

How dare he imply that I was jealous of owlets! Or even interested in him. Especially after what he'd done. I started to say everything I'd stored up for him. "You... you... cad."

He said, "Ouch, steady, next you'll be calling me a bounder."

I said, "That was the next thing I was going to call you."

He laughed and said, "Bloody hell."

I said, "Oh, you think you're so funny, Cain. Telling, telling everyone that I – that I..."

Cain said, "Snogged me?"

I said, "Yes – yes, that and..."

Cain paused and said, "That you liked it?"

I went red. Cain went on. "The thing is, Lullah, whativver I am, I know the truth. I say you liked it. And I know you did."

I couldn't say anything.

He said, "It's true, in't it? You did like it. And this is true as well: I liked it. Very much. And I've kissed a lot of lasses. There you are, that's the truth."

He moved away from the fence and came and stood over me. I looked down. He reached out a gloved hand and lifted my chin up gently so that I had to look him in the eyes. Then he smiled and for a moment looked like a young, good-looking boy.

He said, "You're like some of the deer I feed, all jittery at first, wi' their long legs and big eyes...all nervy. Dun't know whether to come to me or not. Even tho' they get summat nice when they do."

I could feel his warm breath on my face. It smelled of peppermint and a leafy, woody sort of smoky smell. A boy smell.

He said, "Lullah, if it means anything, I didn't mean to upset you at the gig. It's those bloody girls hanging around – them village lasses and the Bottomleys – they do my head in. I say stuff I dun't mean to." He licked his lips slowly and breathed in. "And yeah, it's true I din't like that posh kid telling me to leave off talking to you. Like he was summat special."

I said, "But Cain, you don't even know him. And he's always been nice to me."

Cain laughed. "I know, I said he were a garyboy and I'm right."

I said, "Just because someone is nice doesn't mean they're weak. I like him because he makes me feel good."

Cain said darkly, "Oh aye, and are you saying I dun't?"

I felt a bit hot but also I wanted to stick up for Charlie. I said, "It's nice to have good mates."

Cain said, "I dun't need mates. What would you want mates for?"

Then he paused and went on. "Well, I suppose I dun't really trust anyone. Especially lasses."

I said, "Why?"

He said, "I dunno, they're just trouble."

I said, "Erm, I think you'll find that it's you that's trouble."

But he was somewhere else in his head.

"When I were about nine, me mam said she was going to leave. That she couldn't get on with me dad. And would I go with her."

I'd never seen this side of Cain. I said quietly, "What did you do?"

Cain pushed his hair from his face. "I din't know what she meant, I were too little for that big job. I did me best, I said, 'Dun't go, Mam. I'll talk to me dad and mek him be nicer to you.'"

I said, "And did you?"

Cain laughed. "What were the point? She left that night. And that were that."

I was so shocked I didn't know what to do. I could feel tears in my eyes.

Then Cain shook his hair and said, "Ay up,

that's enough now. This is like one of them TV shows when everyone starts crying and carrying on."

I said, "My mum goes away a lot, but she comes back, usually with an unusual gift. Last time it was a handbag made out of a coconut."

And he laughed. But then there was a long silence.

He took my hand and kissed it. Softly in the palm. Three times. It made my arm go completely to pieces. I wouldn't have been surprised if it had fallen to the ground. He pulled me towards him.

The wind had risen again and was whipping my hair around. I put my free hand up to smooth it down. He caught hold of that hand and said softly, "You're a tender-hearted kitlin, aren't you, miss?"

I closed my eyes. And he very, very slowly brought his lips on to mine. And held them there. Then he put his hands on the side of my face and gave me little soft kisses all along my mouth.

And then down my neck. The wind was blowing, but it was as if we were in one still place.

Suddenly he stopped and said, "Nay, next thing I know you'll be running around after me and Ma Dobbins will get her gun out. Or has she got a bow and arrow?"

I couldn't believe it. What was he doing?

He stepped away from me and whistled for his dog.

I was the one who was supposed to step away not him.

I was furious and said, "Well, as usual, this has been a bundle of laughs. I'm going now. I have many things to do for college."

Cain laughed and said, "I know, lanky lass. I've seen you prancing around like a tit."

I really lost it then. "You might think this is very funny, Cain, but that's because you're a mean person. Who uses other people because you're so..."

Cain said, "Mean? You dun't think I could say anything nice?"

I said, "No, I do not."

He looked me up and down.

"All right, if it's compliments you want.Well… You're a lanky lass, that's true. But you're coming along quite nicely now."

His eyes drifted to the front of my duffel coat. "You know, fattening up in all the right places."

I was speechless. I whirled round and started walking very fast up the path.

I heard Cain shout to his dog, "Come on then, Dog, enough of these lasses."

Just as I got to the bend that led to the village, he called out, "See you later, Lullah. I'll be around. Wait for me. It'll be worth it. You know that really."

I was so shaken up and confused.

He'd actually said I was "fattening up". Like a pig.

I was so angry with him I didn't know what to do with myself.

Him and his dog.

Why doesn't he go out with his dog?

And they could live in a bog.

Or under a log.

He thinks he's er... gog.

No, not gog. God.

I'm going to think of a rap about Cain. It will be my secret artistic revenge on the Dark Black Crow of Heckmondwhite.

When I got to Dandelion Cottage, I couldn't bear to talk to anyone so I said to the Dobbins I'd got a headache and went off to bed.

In my squirrel room, writing in my Darkly Demanding Damson Diary. I can't sleep, so I've been working on my rap or performance poem as I like to call it. Cain gave me a poem so I've got one for him.

You're like a dog
Who lives in a bog
You lurk in the dark
You're a shark

Not a lark
You've got a bone for a heart

So go dig a hole
And hide like a mole
Cos remember they shoot goats, don't they?
Aye
Rastafari.

I must have dozed off but when I woke up it was pitch black outside and I could hear an owl hooting in the distance. It sounded lovely and lonely at the same time. Swooping around in its kingdom. Looking down into the night.

King (or Queen) of the Night.

I wonder if that's why Cain likes them so much.

He'll be up there on the moors somewhere, all dark and wild and on his own.

And here I am on my own.

But he likes being on his own and I don't.

I like being in a gang. I've been on my own too much. But – oh, I don't know.

CHAPTER 19
He's got the right amount of lip

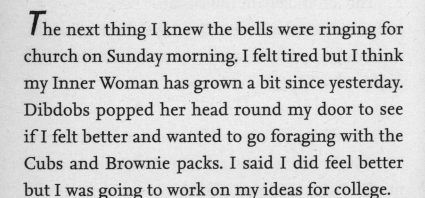

*T*he next thing I knew the bells were ringing for church on Sunday morning. I felt tired but I think my Inner Woman has grown a bit since yesterday. Dibdobs popped her head round my door to see if I felt better and wanted to go foraging with the Cubs and Brownie packs. I said I did feel better but I was going to work on my ideas for college.

As she stomped out in her cagoule, she said, "Well, I'll make a moss cake later to celebrate your art. What larks!"

After I heard the front door slam, I slipped downstairs for a cup of tea and looked through the kitchen window. There were about thirty people all dressed in cagoules in the middle of the green. Is everyone out foraging, I wonder? The woods will be packed. Also, it's all very well collecting fungi and moss, but isn't that what the badgery woodland folk eat? So if we take all their stuff what's left for them? They can't just go and do a big shop, can they?

Anyway, I'm not thinking about it any more. I'm concentrating on my showbiz career. And if I never see Cain again, it will be too soon.

Urrrrgh.

Back in my room. I'm working on an idea for the Taming of the Tights that will knock the socks off Dr Lightowler and her ideas of me being interested in the 'horse genre'.

She doesn't think I have any talent. She thinks that I'm silly, does she?

Well, we'll see about that.

She's going to see a serious side to me.

I can don the golden slippers of applause.

My feet can bleed.

Soooooo I will work on my *Taming of the Shrew* rap.

I'd been making notes and ideas in my Darkly Demanding Damson Diary for about an hour when Ruby and Matilda popped across. They scampered up to see me and Matilda immediately fell asleep on my squirrel bed and started snoring. I wonder what she dreams about. Hoofys probably. Lots of hoofys.

I didn't tell Rubes about the Cain incident, I don't really know how to explain it. He confuses me so much. On one hand I hate him and on the other hand I kissed him and on the other hand, oh, I don't know!!!

How can I know when I've got three hands?!!!

I did tell her about how mean Dr Lightowler is to me. Ruby said, "I could set Matilda on her for you, if you like."

We both looked at Matilda who suddenly sat up and fell off the bed.

I said, "Hmmmmm."

Ruby said, "Have you seen any of the boys? I like Charlie. I think he's well fit. I bet he's reight good at snogging, he's got the right amount of lip."

How does she know that? What is the right amount of lip?

She lugged Matilda back into bed and was still going on about Charlie. "What's more, even after seeing you as a horsey he still likes you."

Yes, that's true. A girl wearing false horse legs is a test, I think.

Ruby was still thinking. "Does he fancy you? Or just like you as a pal?"

Ah, that was the question.

I said, "I don't, well, I don't know. He's got this tiny girlfriend so, well. And also I haven't seen him in ages. I wouldn't know what to do if I did."

Ruby said, "Can't you just like leap on him and snog him until he goes out with you? That's what I'd do."

I bet she would.

She's got Northern grit coming out of her ears.

I wish I had some more.

Rubes went off at one o'clock to have her roast lunch. She had to carry Matilda because she refused to walk.

I worked for another hour and then had a sarnie and looked over what I'd written. Hmmmmm. Right, I've been working on a scene between Petruchio and Kate for the Taming of the Tights. It's like a rap battle between Kate the Shrew and Petruchio.

This is Petruchio's bit. He raps it to Kate when she's dissing him. I've got some spoons to rattle for the beat.

Listen up, sister.
Ayyeeeee.
You no queen
You mean
You not my mate
You my un-mate Kate.
Uh-huh
Oh yeah
Too true
You got a face like a shrew.

Right, this is Kate's rap back.

Me a shrew?
Get you!
Petruchio
You is just a jok-io
Peace
Rastafari
Yo.

Well, it needs a bit of work, but my un-mate Kate is quite good.

When the Dobbins got back, Dibdobs rushed up the stairs to see me. She held out huge lumps of moss. "Oh, Lullah, isn't this fun? I found a cave with enormous supplies of moss. I'm going to make some cakes and I think I'll even have enough left over to try a soup!"

Harold called up the stairs. "Darling, I'm just going to light the fire, we could try toasting some of the snails we found."

I don't think I'll be having tea today. It makes me long for a local sausage and an egg from club-footed Maureen. The boys have just been up to feed the shoe. In its box. Apparently, it likes moss a lot.

From downstairs I could hear Dibdobs laughing in delight and a popping sound. Harold was shouting, "Oooh, there goes another one."

Could that be the snails? It's a massacre of

wildlife down there.

Just then something thudded against my window. Hurray, it's the owlets!!! I opened my window carefully this time and looked down.

Oh goodness gracious, it was Charlie!!

Smiling up at me. He definitely has the phwoar factor.

I said, "Oh, hello, it's you."

He said, "Er, yes, that's what I thought. Lullah, I just happened to be passing, you know, in the dark on a path at the back of your house and I was wondering, even though I've been a bit of a prat, if you'd, you know, try and forgive me. And come on a picnic with me?"

At that point it started hailing. I said, "What, now?"

And we both laughed and he ran round to the front door.

Charlie was so sweet to the Dobbins. He even had a piece of moss cake. And I think he might have been hit by a snail popping out of the fire, but was too nice to say. After five minutes the Dobbins made an excuse to leave us alone in the living room. Dibdobs said, "Well, boys, I think it's time for our story. Shall we go and have our story?"

The twins had been looking and looking at Charlie. Sucking on their dodies.

Dibdobs said, "Split splot, boys, for our story!"

They said, "No story."

But in the end she carried them, still clinging on to Micky and Dicky, up the stairs.

Harold said, "Well, lovely to meet you, Charlie. You may be interested in our Secret Weeping group. Just men together, we go off and talk about our feelings in a secure environment, of course."

Charlie said, "Yes, it sounds very much like Woolfe Academy, Mr Dobbins."

Harold left and Charlie and I laughed.

It was all cosy in front of the fire. I felt warm inside and out. Charlie actually seemed to like me. And I liked him being here. And who'd have thought that I'd have a lovely handsome boy being my friend?

Then we talked about the Cain thing. Even though I was really embarrassed.

Charlie looked into the fire (which luckily wasn't spitting snails, so he wasn't blinded). "Girls really like him, don't they? They like a bad boy."

I started to say, "Well, I can tell you that—"

But he interrupted me and said, "Look, I've got something to say to you – well, something I want to say to you."

I felt a bit nervous.

"I talked to my girlfriend in the holidays – maybe you don't remember her?"

Did I remember his tiny girlfriend??? He wasn't going to get her out of his coat pocket, was he?

"Well, I told her that I thought we were too young to get serious. And that she shouldn't hang around waiting to see me in the holidays. That I needed to be free. And I thought we should both be free."

Wow.

He went on. "I'd better get back to Woolfe now,

but we could go for our picnic next Saturday if you like, about half two if it's not ten feet deep in snow."

Charlie was asking me out on a picnic, my dreams had come true!

Or had they?

Was it a date?

Or, you know, just a picnic?

I said I'd walk as far as the back lane with him and got togged up in my coat. He shouted goodbye to the Dobbins and we went out into the cold.

It was so nice to be with him as we walked along to Beverley's bridge. Although I was nervous. Especially when we accidentally knocked shoulders.

I was thinking. I mean, he'd said that he'd finished with his girlfriend because they should be free. So did that mean he wanted his freedom? And was he just taking me on a picnic in the middle of winter like you would anyone?

Then I remembered what Honey said you had

to do with boys: "Tell the twuth about what you want."

So I took a deep breath and said, "Charlie, you know this picnic? Is it a date?"

Charlie said, "Lullah, are you asking me out on a date?"

I said, "Are you asking *me* on a date?"

He said, "I will if you will."

So I smiled and shook his hand and said, "It's a deal."

So it's a date type date.

Blimey.

And Blinking Nora.

Yaroooo!

Jumping Jehosophat. I am sooo excited about going on a proper date with Charlie I can hardly breathe.

I even ate one of Dibdobs' moss cakes.

And said night-night to the shoe.

That's how happy I was.

CHAPTER 20
Praise the knees!

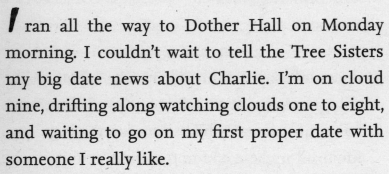

I ran all the way to Dother Hall on Monday morning. I couldn't wait to tell the Tree Sisters my big date news about Charlie. I'm on cloud nine, drifting along watching clouds one to eight, and waiting to go on my first proper date with someone I really like.

The Tree Sisters were almost as excited as me. When I told them about Charlie we did a celebration dance on Vaisey's bed in the dorm.

Flossie said, "Miss Tallulah Mae, you doggone gone and got yourself a boyfriend – it's Jazzle time!" And she got her secret stash out.

Vaisey hugs me every time she sees me.

And even Jo is pleased for me. I know because my arm is black and blue.

This week is going sooooo slowly. It's still only Monday afternoon. I may go mad or have to knock myself out.

The whole of Dother Hall is beavering away at different ideas for the Taming of the Tights. Sidone said, "Girls, I want to involve the WHOLE community. Go out and spread the word far and near. When I told my mature ladies at the Blubberhouses Large Ladies Who Pole Dance For Fun Society, they had some interesting ideas. Some may say pole dancing is the territory of the young and lithe, but that is not their view. I think everyone will be surprised on the night."

When I got back to Heckmondwhite, I bumped into Ruby. She said, "I've thought of something to do for the Taming of the Tights. It will be a mega laugh. Matilda can do some of her backing dancing."

And when I got home, Dibdobs was skipping about the kitchen with joy. "Oh, it will be marvellous. Oooh, Lullah, I could squeeze you!"

She handed me a list of ideas she and Harold had come up with for the Taming of the Tights.

1. *Ethnic drumming*

I know what that will be, a load of pans and a tin bath.

Harold said, "Yes, the Iron Men's Drumming group will search inside themselves for their Inner Woman, and play soft themes of love and harmony on our lovingly crafted drums."

I'd seen his lovingly crafted drum, it is essentially an old dustbin lid.

Then there was Dibdob's special:

2. Foragers' banquet

Dibdobs said, "I suggest a menu of Nettle Soup and Moss Pasta with Wild Garlic and Snails."

Also on their list are:

3. Leaf-hat parades
4. Sheep-poo sculpture competition

On Wednesday I went into Dother Hall and Bob came clinking out of the music studio to put up a notice. It said:

Peace, dudettes

Just a heads up vis-à-vis the Big Night Out. The Iron Pies have got a very extensive playlist for their first outdoor gig. We're gonna rock the forest, man!

Oh dear God, every fool is at it.

On Thursday. Oh, only Thursday, Vaisey came tumbling out of Dother Hall when I arrived.

"Lullah, guess what? The Jones are going to be in the Taming of the Tights!!! Jack said that even Cain was keen. They're using the church hall for rehearsals. They're working on a new song for it."

Cain. I'm not thinking about Cain.

Ever again.

He's a pain.

Hang on, I'm making a mental rap about him. No! Stop.

And anyway, I've much better things to do. I'm preparing myself for MY DATE with Charlie. I've never had an actual date with a real boy before. Floppy Ben doesn't count.

And Charlie's gorgeous. Everyone says he's gorgeous. I think he's gorgeous. I bet even Matilda thinks he's gorgeous.

That's cos he's gorgeous.

As I left to walk home, Flossie came and linked

up with me. She was wearing loads of make-up. I said, "What are you doing?"

She smiled at me. Bit scary.

"Do you know, Lulles, I think I'll walk you into Heckmondwhite. I don't want those big rough Bottomleys bothering you."

I said, "Er, they bother me all the time. But it's usually just staring these days."

When we got to the village, Flossie wouldn't let me go home. She made me walk around the church hall about a million times. After the fourth time I realised – she just wants to see Seth. But the band didn't turn up and by six o'clock I was freezing. And also I didn't want to be around if Cain turned up, so I said I was going home.

Then Flossie said, "Oh yeah, good idea but I couldn't go home without seeing little Rubester. I really miss her and want to talk to her. A lot."

So she dragged me round to The Blind Pig.

Flossie hugged Ruby and said, "Hello Ruby, nice to see you. It's been ages."

And then we all went up to Ruby's room to "catch

up" as Flossie said.

Ruby started telling us about Matilda's backing dancing and Joey the boy she used to snog. But then Ruby noticed that Flossie was looking out of the window, saying, "Ah-huh" to anything she said.

In the end, Ruby said, "Is it true that you only have one corker?"

When Flossie did her "Ah-huh", Ruby went over and looked her in the face and said, "They're not rehearsing tonight."

Flossie immediately got up and said, "S'laters."

At last it's Saturday. Date day!!

Rubes insisted on spending all morning helping me get ready. I don't know who is more excited and nervous: me, Ruby or Matilda. Ruby was going through my things saying, "You want to be snug, but not look like a long sock."

Yes, that's true.

I made her go home at two o'clock because I

didn't want her lurking around when Charlie came. She was not pleased.

"I'm not a kid you know."

I said, "You are actually."

She went in the end, but she said, "It's a free country, I might fancy being around your house or something later on."

I said, "Please don't."

As she was sulking off, she said, "Anyway, I think that Charlie fancies me really."

She is truly unbalanced. In a nice way.

I'm all ready, but it's freezing, so I'm going to get into bed again. I can't be bothered to take my jeans off. I'll stay snug until he arrives.

Or not arrives. Maybe he's changed his mind.

I felt really jittery and a bit sick.

Then, just on two-thirty, Dibdobs called up. "Lullah, Charlie's here!!"

I sjuuugged my hair and put some Pouty Pink lip gloss on and another quick layer of mascara. Like I learned from Cousin Georgia.

There's a funny smell all over the house.

Harold must be trying out more eco-friendly heating materials. He's outdone himself this time because there's a slight whiff of piggy poo from the downstairs fire.

Surely you can't burn piggy poo?

And anyway what fool would.

I squirted myself with perfume. Deep breaths and then a practice smile in the mirror. What did Georgia say to me?

"Oh yes, little cousy, the secret to smiling at a boy is 'a hint of eastern promise' but not full-on 'I'm a tart'."

I think I know what she means.

As I got to the top of the wooden stairs, I could hear the lunatic twins talking to Charlie.

Charlie said, "It's quite big, isn't it, Sam?"

And Sam saying, "It's sjuuuge."

And Max said, "Sjuuuge shoe."

Oh dear.

They were showing him the shoe.

When I went into the kitchen, smoke was billowing from the fire. Sort of dark brown smoke. With a piggy aroma. Dibdobs was showing Charlie an egg with a hat on that she's designed for the Taming of the Tights.

Charlie smiled his Charlie smile when he saw me. He had a dark blue coat on and his thick wavy hair touched the collar. My knees went a bit trembly, but there was nothing they could do as I had trapped them into thermal leggings under my jeans.

Charlie said, "Hello, gorgeous. It's parky, isn't it? But I thought we could go out owl hunting for a bit, if you fancy it? If it's OK to come out?"

And he looked at Dibdobs who was knitting more egg hats.

She's not hatching them, is she?

The eggs, I mean, not the hats. Although you never know.

She clicked her needles and said, "Yes, yes, you young people, off you go. Wrap up snug, Lullah, put your big coat on, it's in the cupboard."

I put my coat on and then Max and Sam put their little arms round my legs. We shuffled off towards the door as a group. They only let go when I gently shut the door on them. As he disappeared behind it, Sam said, "Ug oo."

Charlie was laughing as he pulled up his collar against the cold air. "Erm, are they a bit on the odd side?"

I said, "You should see them in their leaf hats."

He laughed again as we went out of the gate. "This is fun, Lullah. Nice to see you. I thought we could go to the woods and see if we can find the feathery fools and have our picnic there."

I said, "I'm very much looking forward to our picnic. It's just the weather for an outdoor meal."

Charlie said, "I'd better get used to outdoor meals. We're off on a country skills camping week in Scotland on Monday. Still, we'll learn to track a wild pig. So that's, you know, something."

As we went down the back path, I heard a bit of a snuffle. Without turning round, I shouted, "Goodbye, Ruby."

Ruby came out of the bushes with Matilda. She said, "I weren't following you or owt. Matilda wanted to... to... see Charlie."

Charlie bent down and kissed Matilda on the nose. She wagged her stump.

Ruby said, "What about me?"

So Charlie gave her a big kiss on her nose too.

She said, "Cor, I were right, you have got just the right amount of lip."

Charlie said, "Well, thank you, that's a relief."

Matilda and Ruby scampered off.

As we tramped down the back path, it was crunchy and silvery beneath our feet. You could see your breath in the air before you. I hunched my shoulders and shivered. Charlie said, "Are you cold?"

I said, "No, no, I'm sooo, you know, just a bit, well, you know, excited really. I feel like, like a dog shaking its back leg."

There was a pause as Charlie looked at me.

I thought, *Why did I say that thing about the dog leg?*

Charlie said, "Yep, that is exciting indeed."

I smiled at him. I can feel the warmth coming

from him, sort of all over. The dark trees rustled with a sudden tremor of wind from the moors and I shook my hair.

"You know it's nearly the Taming of the Tights bonfire thing and there's something in the air and you can just feel that something really exciting and great is going to happen."

Charlie suddenly stopped, so I did too. He was looking at me without saying anything. He has such smiley eyes. Eyes that say, "Hello."

Should I blink or would that make him stop looking at me?

I wish I could remember what you were supposed to do. What was it Cousin Georgia said? Look up and then look down? And then you look up again?

I tried that. After I'd done it twice, Charlie said, "Have you got something in your eye?"

He stroked my face.

Wow. This was it.

He said, "Your eyes are really green. They're amazing."

But then we heard hooting off towards the old barn and he said, "That might be them – that might be the owlets!"

And we ran towards the barn calling "Twit twoo, little Lullah and little Ruby."

We went into the dark old barn with its creaky door. Patches of pale light were beaming on to the hay from the broken roof. Charlie said, "Blimey, this brings back memories, doesn't it? You doing your owlet impression, me lying on the ground."

I said, "Charlie, a lot of water has passed under the bridge since then, basically, I am not an idiot child any more."

Charlie said, "Er, can you just remind me of the rap you did as a horse?"

I laughed. He did have a point.

There was no sign of the owlets. But it was cosy and out of the biting wind in the barn. I said, "Ooh, I'm a bit peckish. Shall we have our lovely picnic now?"

Charlie said, "Oh yes, I hope you're hungry." And he got out two bags of salt and vinegar crisps.

I laughed and said, "Is that it?"

He said, "Don't be silly, Lullah. There's a Kit Kat for afters. I know how to show a girl a good time."

It was fun sitting together on the hay bale. Not just like sharing a Kit Kat with a girl chum. You don't generally want your girl chum to kiss you after finishing their Kit Kat.

I wonder if he will kiss me.

Charlie lounged back in the hay. I tried lounging as well. Through the open barn door we could see the stars beginning to appear.

There was light enough to see his face clearly. I peeked a sideways look at him. He really is good-looking and has a lovely mouth. He turned to me a bit seriously. I wonder if he was thinking that I had a nice mouth.

Charlie said, "I know you're not an idiot child, Lullah, but I have to ask you, just to get it out in the open. Why on earth would you get involved with someone like Cain? He's such, well... an arse. Isn't he?"

I nodded. "Well, yeah, he is."

Charlie went on. "He's rude, he's moody, he's violent, he's mean. No one likes him. Well, apart from, you know, some girls."

I said quickly, "Charlie, I know what he is. He's awful, he does awful things. He IS awful. I call him the Dark Black Crow of Heckmondwhite. No one in their right mind would have anything to do with Cain. I just made a mistake, but it won't happen again."

As I said that, there was the crack of a twig outside and a rustling and I thought I heard the beating of wings. The owlets!

We both went round the side of the barn, but there was nothing there. They must have flown off. Up into the branches.

It was chilly. I shivered. Maybe Charlie would notice and put his arm around me.

He said, "Let's walk a bit."

I said, "I could show you the sheep."

Charlie laughed. "Great."

As we walked, he put his hands in his pockets and said, "Yeah, I don't like Cain, but I can see that when he's in his band, I suppose he's, well, he's sexy, isn't he? He's sort of wild."

I said, "Like an animal in trousers."

Charlie laughed. "Exactly. But that's all he is. He's not going to suddenly stop and be a laugh and nice to you. You know that, don't you?"

We walked on for a bit then Charlie said, "Lullah, you're a bit wild and out of control – well, your legs are."

I said, "I know."

We both looked down at my legs.

If they start doing anything now, I'll kill them.

Charlie said, "But I like them."

And he took my hand in his and put them both in his pocket. It's really nice and warm in there. And there's no tiny girlfriend involved.

Charlie went on. "Lullah, you're different. You're sort of exciting and mad at the same time. And I like it."

We reached the sheep field and stopped to lean on the fence. Looking at the sheep chewing on stuff. Looking at us. And then they did that thing again. They started trying to get into the hedge.

Charlie said, "Why are they doing that?"

I said, "I don't know. I sang *The Sound of Music* to them and now every time they see me they get into the hedge."

Charlie started laughing so much I thought he might not be able to stop. It made me laugh as well. And he hugged me to him.

"God, Lullah, you are just... well... gorgeous."

I leant to rest against the fence and swished my hair back. I looked up at the stars. Charlie spoke softly but quite intensely. "What I want you to know is..."

And he put both of his hands around my face and looked down at me. "Wow, Lulles, look at you, all catty in the night. Your eyes are proper green. You think that you're vulnerable and you are, but that's what's so nice. No wonder Cain wants you."

I closed my eyes. I actually felt a bit dizzy.

This was one of the dreamiest things that had ever happened to me. Then he put his hands behind my back and tried to pull me in towards him. But my hair was caught in the thorn hedge. In between laughing, Charlie managed to tug my hair free. It still felt a bit knotty.

Charlie was smiling as he caught hold of me again. He leaned down and softly kissed me on the lips.

Wow. I'm melting.

He kissed me softly again and then a bit harder. And as he was kissing me, he ran his hand through the back of my hair.

"Bloody hell, Lullah, there's half a hedge in your hair. Look!" And he showed me a twig.

And then he put his hands back in his pockets and looked at me quite seriously and said, "So here's the thing. You know I like you. And what I need to know is who you prefer – me or you know who."

Charlie blew me a kiss as he walked away. I stood at the gate in a daze, watching him go. As he disappeared up the path to Woolfe Academy, he shouted, "Praise the knees!"

CHAPTER 21

Fir-cone earrings and knitted onesies

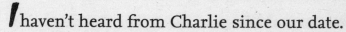

I haven't heard from Charlie since our date.

It's Sunday afternoon. No note. No accidental meeting in the lane going to the barn. Even though I have pretty much lurked around there since we left it last night. The sheep are still getting into the hedge. I even tried bobbing down behind the fence so they couldn't see me approaching, but they seem to sense my presence.

I wonder why he hasn't been in touch. Should I

be doing something?

Everything is hotting up for the Taming of the Tights extravaganza. On Thursday, the Tree Sisters were in our official meeting place in the dorm. Once again snuggled up in Vaisey's bed, talking about boys.

I said, "I really like Charlie and I want to see him."

Jo said, "So why don't you tell him?"

I said, "I would if I could see him."

Flossie said, "Charlie Farlie, how you girls do prattle on. I'm going to give that young man Seth a chance to make it up to me at The Taming of the Tights. Why, I feel downright mean and I done think he's suffered enough not seeing me."

I said, "Ruby said he was hanging around the churchyard with some of the village girls last night."

Flossie said, "He'll be trying to keep his spirits up."

I said, "Well, you snogged Batboy in front of him, tore up his poster and didn't meet him when he said he'd see you after the gig."

Flossie said, "I know. It's all going to plan, isn't it?"

What?

All week, the Dobbins kitchen has been a nightmare of preparation for The Taming of the Tights. Dibdobs and her village foraging group have been baking moss and mushroom tarts and freezing them for the last three days. And I've never seen so many conker bracelets and fir-cone earrings.

Dibdobs has moved on from knitting egg hats to knitted onesies for animals. Micky and Dicky are wearing theirs. But not their mittens. So far Dibdobs hasn't managed to get them on.

It's the Taming of the Tights eve and it's like being in a mad washing machine at Dother Hall: people racing around in costumes, cut-out trees being carted about, doors dropping off. Practically everything is broken because Bob spends all his time rehearsing with The Iron Pies. The only constant thing is that Dr Lightowler is looking madder by the minute.

I said to Vaisey, "Ooh, look, Dr Lightowler has made a nest in the dance studio."

And Vaisey actually looked up to the rafters.

It was hard to get to sleep that night because I know Charlie will be back tomorrow.

CHAPTER 22
The Taming of the Tights

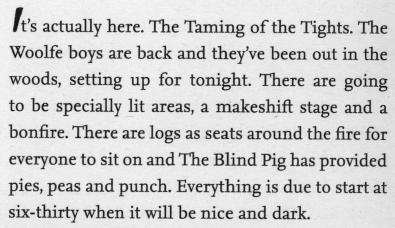

*I*t's actually here. The Taming of the Tights. The Woolfe boys are back and they've been out in the woods, setting up for tonight. There are going to be specially lit areas, a makeshift stage and a bonfire. There are logs as seats around the fire for everyone to sit on and The Blind Pig has provided pies, peas and punch. Everything is due to start at six-thirty when it will be nice and dark.

Bob has made fire torches to light people's way

through the woods to the bonfire.

Jo said, "I helped him make them, so I think if we call the fire brigade nice and early, perhaps about five forty-five, there's a good chance that some of the forest can be saved."

In the dance studio at five, Monty gave us a pre-performance pep talk. He was very excited.

"This is our chance to show our neighbours the magic of theatre and performance. It's going to be marvellous. A cornucopia of musick, dance, love, food. Sidone and I will do our wedding feast dance scene; the lovers united at last. And we have a special little surprise for you."

We all looked at each other and Monty tapped his nose. Flossie said, "He's not going to wear his pink onesie, is he?"

Monty went on. "Music galore! The Iron Pies. The Jones. Harold and his Iron Men's drumming group. This night is going to be one to remember. No one who sees it will ever forget it."

We were all excited. But me especially. I would be seeing Charlie again. I've been thinking about what I'm going to say to him all week.

I couldn't imagine what was going to happen next. Normally, I can imagine everything: pantaloons, shrew bands, flouncy shirts, being a shrew. But when I think of actually being Charlie's girlfriend...

We got changed into our costumes in the dorm. Flossie and Jo got togged up in their jesters costumes. Flossie was practising her juggling and Jo was hitting us with her rubber dumbells. I was wearing a floor-length purple velvet coat over my green tights. Dibdobs said that the coat had belonged to her great-grandmother. It felt lovely.

Vaisey had helped me with my Kate make-up. She said, "I'm going to do a sort of silvery purple line around your eyes. I think you'll look really lovely."

Even Lav, Dav and Noos wafting about practising their songs as 'The Biancas' couldn't annoy me.

When it was time to set off to the bonfire, I gave my Tree Sisters a big hug. I yelled, "We are all showing our inner glorwee, just as Honey told us to!!! Yaroooo!"

The stars came out early and it was like being in an enchanted forest. The woods were heaving with people. Young and old and Mr Barraclough. The Iron Pies were there dressed up in Viking horns and long cloaks. When we got to the main clearing, Ruby came scampering up with Matilda.

Matilda had her leather cap and a ra-ra skirt on. Ruby was also wearing a leather cap and a ra-ra skirt.

She said, "Ay up, Tree Sisters!!! There's some hot totty here tonight. They're going to be well impressed wi' me and Matilda's backing dancing."

More and more people came. They were sitting on the logs and piling into the pies and peas and punch. Bob started testing his drum kit on the stage.

I looked at him and said, "I've never seen anyone wearing sunglasses at night in November before."

Flossie said, "You have now."

It was exciting, but there was no sign of Charlie.

Then we heard hunting horns and the Woolfe boys came rollicking into the clearing. Hoppy was trying to keep order.

"Boys, boys, don't let yourselves down. Remember all we have as men are our reputations so we should... Oh now, boys is that taken from the kitchen supplies?"

Phil snuck up on Jo and whispered, "It's a Sausage Guy Fawkes. We went on a sausage raid. It's made out of three hundred pork sausages."

We all started laughing. The sausage man even had dreadlocks made out of sausages. Phil said, "It's our tribute to your rapping, Lullah."

I felt proud. What larks!

The only thing missing was Charlie.

I asked Phil where he was and Phil said, "Well, he was at Woolfe when I left, sorting out the fire buckets – we're the fire monitors. Hoppy said we need a more mature attitude to fire."

I said, "Did Charlie mention me?"

Phil looked at me. "Aaaah, you like him, don't you?"

I went a bit red but couldn't help smiling. Jo threw herself on to Phil's back and made him giddy up as her horsey so I couldn't ask him anything else. Then Vaisey said, "Oh, they're here!"

But Ruben and Jack walked into the clearing. Jack was carrying a tom-tom drum.

I said to Vaisey, "Vaisey, please for once will you not tell me about Jack's new sticks? I'm feeling a bit nervous."

Vaisey said, "No, he's gone native tonight, he's stickless. He's going to use his hands. He's got lovely hands."

There was no sign of Seth or Cain, which was an enormous relief. I hadn't been able to think about what it would be like for Cain and Charlie to be in the same place. I couldn't help remembering what had happened last time.

Where was Charlie?

Had he had time to think things over whilst he was tracking wild pigs? Had he thought, do I really want a girlfriend who frightens sheep, has uncontrollable legs and puts her head in thorn hedges? Or do I want a normal girlfriend?

The festivities began with the lighting of the bonfire. As it burst into flame, Gudrun, in what looked like a knitted elf costume, was dithering on the stage in front of the audience. She shouted above the cheering, "Erm, could you all... Would you very much mind I don't think that putting the sausage man on the bonfire is very sensible... Boys! Oh dear. Anyway... I..."

Eventually Mr Barraclough shouted, with a pie in each hand, "Shut it, lads, I've got an announcement. Our thespian friends are about to prance around like fools for our entertainment."

And Gudrun said, "Yes, yes, thank you. I proudly present our inspirational headmistress Ms Sidone Beaver as Petruchio and our revered theatrical tutor Monty de Courcy as Kate, in our own Dother Hall version of the war of the sexes in... The Taming of the Tights!"

Everyone shouted and whistled and The Iron Pies played a bit of *The Long and Winding Tights* as Sidone and Monty entered the clearing.

Sidone was wearing a flouncy shirt and breeches and a small beard, and Monty was in a crinoline and curly wig. They hid behind different trees and began the wedding feast speeches from *The Taming of the Shrew*.

We felt the love immediately. Sidone grasped Monty roughly around the waist and clasped him to her flouncy shirt. Monty looked thrilled.

One of the village lads yelled out, "You lucky, lucky man, she's GORGEOUS!" Monty held his fan to his face and adjusted his crinoline. His Inner Woman was quite literally bursting out.

At the end of the wedding scene, Sidone trapped Monty against Bob's drum kit on the stage in a final embrace. The audience were cheering and whistling, but Bob shouted, "Cool your boots, dudes!" and leapt out to protect his kit.

The lads from The Blind Pig practically fell over they were laughing so much as Sidone and

Monty bowed for about ten minutes.

I was laughing with my Tree Sisters. But still no sign of Charlie.

Then The Jones, well, Ruben and Jack, joined in with The Iron Pies for *Sky-tights* and *From Russia with Tights*.

Where was Seth? Where was Cain?

And where was Charlie?

I hope they haven't bumped into each other on their way here. I was distracted by Matilda's backing dancing which was... er... mostly Ruby moving Matilda's front legs to the rhythm. The ra-ra skirts and caps looked nice though.

Then there was a fashion show of day to evening foraging wear, featuring a leaf-hat parade modelled by the Little Foragers' Club and a range of fir-cone earrings and conker wear modelled by Dibdobs and the Blubberhouses Large Ladies Who Pole Dance For Fun Society. Harold made a guest appearance in a pair of moss trousers which clearly weren't going to last the night.

In between acts, Flossie and Jo as the jesters

entertained the crowd with tights juggling and random acts of violence. Jo caught Mr Legge a glancing blow with her rubber dumbbells. And knocked him into the sheep-poo sculptures.

Then it was time for me and Vaisey to do our Shrew Rap battle.

As we waited to go on, I said to Vaisey, "Charlie's still not here. I really wanted him to see me do something good."

Vaisey squeezed my hand.

And then we were on.

Dr Lightowler came out of the shadows to watch. Bob and Jack started a beat on the same drum.

Flossie shouted, "Here's the hard man Petruchio!"

Vaisey swaggered on stage in her tights and moustache. She was quite scary for someone who is actually a very nice person. The crowd whooped.

Then Jo shouted, "And here's Queen of Hate, Kate!"

And I stamped on and clicked my fingers in Petruchio's face. The crowd started clapping along with the beat of the drum.

The rap battle began. Vaisey rapped:

"Listen up, sister Kate
Before it too late
You no Queen
You mean
Uh-huh
Too true
You got a face like a shrew."

And she slapped my face. Quite hard.

I was a bit annoyed that Vaisey's Inner Man had probably left a hand-shaped mark on my cheek. So I gave it my all.

I stalked around moodily, looking at the crowd. Kissing my teeth and pointing at random people.

Including Dr Lightowler.

I even kicked Bob's drums. He came and stood in front of them. I put my hands on my hips and began my Kate rap:

"Me a shrew?
Get you!
Call yourself Petruchio
You is just a joke-io
Clear off unless you want a poke-io
Peace
Rastafari
Yo."

Then Jack started playing a hiddly diddly on his drum. My knees couldn't resist and I flung aside my coat and released my legs.

My spontaneous Irish dancing was a huge hit with the crowd. Everyone was whooping and cheering and we had to take three bows.

Blaise was jumping up and down, and Sidone said to me as I came off stage, "Being funny is the hardest thing. Listen to your golden slippers of applause. I've always said there's something really, really unusual about you, Tallulah."

I'm a star, I'm a star!!! I'm a...

Seth stepped into the light from out of the

trees. He went straight over to Flossie who was talking to Ben.

Seth tapped Ben on the shoulder and said, "Here's ten pence, young lad, go and get yourself a sausage."

And then he got hold of Flossie and snogged her so much the bells on her jester's hat started ringing. The Woolfe sports master went over and tapped Seth on the shoulder, saying, "Now then, young man, none of that business here."

Seth stopped kissing Flossie and got another ten pence out of his pocket. "Get yourself a sausage as well, little lad."

Amazing.

The Bottomley sisters turned up and evilled me as they headed for the pies and peas stall.

Then, Cain appeared. All in black. He glanced at me. And winked. How dare he!!

Beverley turned back to talk to him but then a minute later she ran off crying into the woods.

Jack and Ruben started playing the *I'm your darkest nightmare but it's me you want* song on stage.

Seth got his guitar and joined in the rhythm. Bob handed Cain a mike and he started singing.

> *"Bad luck and trouble*
> *Are my middle name*
> *If you were me, you would be the same*
> *Hey now, baby, why dun't you come with me*
> *I want to show you how very bad I can be."*

I'm not listening to this any more. I turned away, and there was Charlie.

He said, "Hello, Tallulah."

I said, "Hello, Charlie."

I felt shy. I didn't know what to say.

Charlie said, "This is nice." Then he looked down. "You, me and your knees."

That did make me laugh. The Jones were still playing but I didn't notice. I was so glad Charlie was here.

Charlie said, "Sorry I wasn't here earlier. Did I miss your rap battle?"

I said, "Yeah, I got the golden slippers of applause."

Charlie stroked his hand through my hair then said, "Oh, hang on, there's nothing sharp in here, is there?"

And we both laughed.

As we did, the music crashed to a halt. Cain shouted at the crowd. "Settle down, I've got summat to show thee. I've trained some birds for the party. Because, as you know, I'm good with birds."

And he looked up from underneath his eyelashes at me and Charlie. I looked away.

Mr Barraclough shouted, "Come on then, Cain, show us your bird trick!"

Cain made a clicking sound, and when I looked up little Lullah swooped down from the darkness on to his head! Cain made another click and little Ruby appeared and hopped on to his shoulder.

Ruby shouted, "Halloooo, little owlets!"

Cain clicked again and little Lullah hopped on to his other shoulder. The two owlets started nibbling his ears. Not pecking him. It looked like they were kissing his ears.

Cain said, "You see, ladies and gentlemen, birds

like to do what I tell them."

And he looked slyly across at me.

I looked up at Charlie but I couldn't read his expression. He just had his arms folded, watching.

Cain clicked at the owlets again and they swooped on to Ted's horns. People applauded.

Ted said, "Bloody hell, I hope there are no unfortunate toilet accidents on my new horns."

It was really wild being in the middle of the wood with the fire burning and the owlets preening and puffing themselves up.

Cain bent down to a bag he'd placed at his feet and took something out. He said, "They say we know nowt about art in Heckmondwhite, that we're savages. But tonight I give you Yorkshire's version of *The Taming of the Shrews.*"

A few people clapped. He opened his hands. Vaisey said, "Aaah, look, he's got two little shrews!"

Cain smiled and said, "Reight cute, aren't they? Let's let 'em free." He dropped them on the floor and the shrews started scuttling off.

Cain clicked his tongue and little Lullah and Ruby flashed down from Ted's horns and on to the shrews, caught them in their talons and swooped off into the forest.

Cain smiled his dark smile and bowed.

Half of the crowd clapped.

Charlie said, "That bloke is an idiot."

As he said that, there was a massive explosion from the bonfire. We looked around to see flaming sausages hurtling through the air. Charlie said, "Oh God, Sausage Man!" And dashed off towards the bonfire.

Everyone, including the Tree Sisters, went to see what was happening.

Then I heard Cain's voice behind me. "All right, lanky lass, enjoy the show?"

I turned round. I was shaking. I said, "You horrible murderer."

Cain said, "Me? I think you'll have to speak to the owlets about that."

I didn't mean to but I was so shocked I started to cry.

Cain said, "Stop carrying on. What's wrong with you?"

I said, "You're so brutal... everything you do is so cruel."

He said, "Is it? Mebbe I understand more than you think. Them owlets that you love so much – they're not pets. They dun't eat salad. They eat meece and shrews and grubs. That's their nature. They're wild."

I couldn't speak to him.

He went on. "And why should I care what you think? I know you hate me. I overheard you and Garyboy talking about me in the barn."

It had been him. The noise Charlie and I had heard.

Oh.

"But for all that, you and I know there's summat between us. I want to kiss you and you want to kiss me."

Cain pulled me to him suddenly. And as he looked at me with his dark wild eyes he brought his mouth down on mine.

But the Dark Black Crow of Heckmondwhite really doesn't know what I want.

I pushed him away from me and walked back to the bonfire.

When I got there, the Sausage Man was under control. Charlie was talking to Phil. He saw me and smiled. His lovely Charlie smile.

I smiled back.

Charlie came over and took my hand. And without saying anything we walked to the Tree Sisters Special Tree.

When we got there, Charlie let go of my hand and leaned against it. "This is where it all began, didn't it? I sort of knew when I first saw you that…"

He looked into my eyes and said, "Come here."

He pulled me closer and got hold of the lapels of my velvet coat. He was taller than me and as he lifted me up I stood on my tippy toes. My mouth was very near his. He said softly, "Don't be worried. You'll see, Lullah, this'll be good between us."

Then he actually picked me up so I was looking down at him.

He smiled. "Hello there. I've thought about this a lot. About doing this."

And he let me down slowly, until our lips touched.

He brushed my lips softly with his. I shut my eyes and felt the lovely softness. It was like being half asleep and yet really alive. He started kissing me more and he put his hands on the base of my spine. And I couldn't help it, my mind said, *Yep, that's the right place to put hands, just above the sticky-out bit.*

My brain froze as he kissed me in little waves. Some of them very soft and some a bit harder. He pressed his hands all up my spine as he kissed me.

And I just completely lost myself in it. Every bit of me felt connected to the kiss. He put the tip of his tongue between my lips and softly stroked it across the inside of my upper lip and then my lower lip. I could have stayed there kissing him forever.

Charlie smiled down at me and ran his hands through my hair, then said, "Well, that was good for a start wasn't it, miss?"

I couldn't speak I was so happy. He put his arms round me.

He said, "So is it me or the shrew murderer?"

I said, "It's you."

He nodded. "Very wise."

And he bent down and kissed me again on the mouth. Then he said to me, "Wow, this is going to be good."

And kissed me again.

So all's well that ends well. And I do mean that.

When we got back to the bonfire everyone was dancing and laughing.

Seth put Flossie over his shoulder and danced about with her, and then Flossie put Seth over her shoulder.

Vaisey and Jack did a drum duet.

Jo and Phil were taking turns to hit each other with the rubber dumbbells.

And whilst The Biancas (Lav, Dav and Noos) were singing *Isn't she lovely*, Dil Bottomley had Ben pinned against a tree.

And Hoppy?

Hoppy was showing Blaise his hopping.

But, best of all, a flaming sausage had ignited Dr Lightowler's cloak and Bob had to wrestle her to the ground and beat it out with his special fire blanket.

After we said goodbye to our boyfriends, the Tree Sisters and me walked back to Dother Hall, arm in arm.

Flossie said, "Girls, I am so goddammed pooped. I got up to Number 6 on the Lulu-luuuve List with an animal in trousers."

Vaisey said, "Ooooh, well, Jack had to play the drums all night, so mostly we, well, mostly we did Number 2."

We all hugged her and said, "Aw, that's a shame."

But Vaisey hadn't finished.

She said, "But when everyone was eating their sausages we got to Number 6."

Jo punched Vaisey on the arm and said, "Rock on, sister! Phil and I never stopped doing Number 6 all night!"

There was a little silence then Vaisey squeezed my arm and said, "Did you...? Did Charlie...? Erm... did you get on the Lulu-luuuve List?"

I took a deep breath then said, "What comes after five?"

And me and my Tree Sisters danced all the way back to our theatre of dreams.

Later, in my squirrel bed, I heard a scrabbling at the window. When I looked out, the owlets were there. Looking at me.

I can't help loving them. And I know they love me in their own wild way.

But they need to be wild and free.

Just like Cain.

They flew off into the darkness. And I snuggled down again and fell asleep, thinking about my lovely Charlie.

My first proper boyfriend.

OUT NOW

Winner of The Roald Dahl FUNNY PRIZE

Louise Rennison

Bestselling author of the Georgia Nicolson series

WITHERING TIGHTS

the misadventures of Tallulah Casey

SEE HOW IT ALL BEGAN FOR TALLULAH OVER THE PAGE...

The Corker-holding with
winter socks scene

Where's that James Bond book Dad gave me? Here it is.

Now where did I get to?

Oh yes. In Jamaica, it's the bit where Honeychile is so hot and the fans are going round and round in the hotel room. And the waves are crashing against the shore. And so Honeychile took off all her clothes and stood by the window. Yes, this is the good bit.

Bond went across to her and took a breast in each hand. But still she looked away from him out of the window.

"Not now," she said in a low voice.

How does that work? Is that what you're supposed to do? Should I have said "Not now" to Ben?

If I act it out, I might get an idea of what it feels like.

I won't take off my jim-jams, I will just imagine that bit.

Although it's hard to imagine someone putting their hands over my corkers as I haven't really got any.

Maybe if I put socks down the front of my jim-jams that would be more like corkers. Yes, but then I wouldn't know what it felt like to have a hand over each one.

Maybe, if I put the socks on my hands, that would give me more of an idea.

I'll use my big thick hiking ones.

OK.

Right, I am walking in a sexy way to the window. Phew, I am hot. I am imagining the Caribbean Sea crashing against the shed at the bottom of the garden. James Bond coming over to me. He is putting a hand over each breast. Oooh, the hiking socks are a bit prickly. I am looking away from him out of the window. I am saying, "Not now..."

Oh, dear Virgin Mary and all her cohort, there is someone down there looking up at me!!! I bobbed down beneath the windowsill.

The light was on in my room.

Had they seen me fondling myself with hiking socks??

I stayed absolutely still.

Perhaps they hadn't seen anything and were just looking at owls or...

A voice shouted up. "Have you gone all shy now? Why don't tha come out and play with me?"

And a girl's voice further away said, "You think you're something."

And the boy said, "Correction, love, I KNOW I'm something. I'm Cain Hinchcliff."

———

Also Available:

Bestselling author of the Georgia Nicolson series

Louise Rennison

A MIDSUMMER TIGHTS DREAM

more (boy snogging) misadventures of Tallulah Casey

Georgia's Ace Gang Snogging Scale

$1/4$. kissing hands

$1/2$. sticky eyes *(Be careful using this. I've still got some complete twit following me around like a seeing-eye dog.)*

1. holding hands

2. arm around

3. goodnight kiss

4. kiss lasting over three minutes without a break *(What you need for this is a sad mate who's got a watch but no boyfriend.)*

$41/2$. hand snogging *(I really don't want to go into this. Ask Jas.)*

5. open mouth kissing

6. tongues

$61/2$. ear snogging

$63/4$. neck nuzzling

7. upper-body fondling - outdoors

8. upper-body fondling - indoors

Virtual number 8. *(When your upper body is not actually being fondled in reality, but you know that it is in your snoggees head.)*

9. below waist activity *(Or b.w.a.)*

10. the full monty *(Jas and I were in the room when Dad was watching the news and the newscaster said, "Tonight the Prime Minister has reached Number 10." And Jas and I had a laughing spaz to end all laughing spazzes.)*

Want to meet Tallulah's
cheeky cousin Georgia?

Read the fabbity-fab
CONFESSIONS OF GEORGIA NICOLSON

1

NUMBER ONE BESTSELLING AUTHOR
Angus, thongs and full-frontal snogging
You'll laugh your knickers off!
Louise Rennison

2

NUMBER ONE BESTSELLING AUTHOR
'It's OK, I'm wearing really big knickers!'
Fabulously funny!
Louise Rennison

3

FABULOUSLY FUNNY BESTSELLER
'Knocked out by my nunga-nungas.'
You'll laugh your knickers off!
Louise Rennison

4

NUMBER ONE BESTSELLING AUTHOR
'Dancing in my nuddy-pants!'
You'll laugh your knickers off!
Louise Rennison

Go on, you know you want to!

'...and that's when it fell off in my ♥ hand.'

You'll laugh your knickers off!

Louise Rennison ♥

'...then he ate my ♥ boy entrancers.'

You'll laugh your knickers off!

Louise Rennison ♥

'...startled by his furry shorts!' ♥

Fab New Confessions of Georgia Nicolson

Louise Rennison ♥

'Luuurve is a many trousered thing...'

Fab New Confessions of Georgia Nicolson

Louise Rennison ♥

'Stop in the ♥ name of pants!'

Fab New Confessions of Georgia Nicolson

Louise Rennison ♥

'Are these my basoomas I see before me?' ♥

Fab FINAL Confessions of Georgia Nicolson

Louise Rennison ♥

Voted No. 1 Queen of Teen

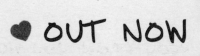

♥ OUT NOW